# JANE AUSTEN'S

# PRIDE *and* PREJUDICE

# AWESOMELY AUSTEN
*Illustrated by Églantine Ceulemans*

*

*

*

*

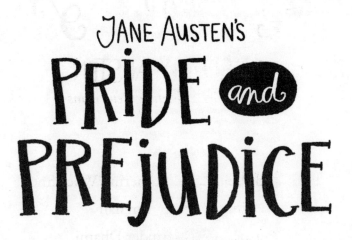

Jane Austen's
# PRIDE and PREJUDICE

RETOLD BY KATHERINE WOODFINE
ILLUSTRATED BY ÉGLANTINE CEULEMANS

HODDER

First published in Great Britain in 2019 by Hodder and Stoughton

1 3 5 7 9 10 8 6 4 2

Text copyright © Katherine Woodfine, 2019
Illustrations copyright © Églantine Ceulemans, 2019

The moral right of the author has been asserted.

A CIP catalogue record for this book
is available from the British Library.

ISBN 978 1 444 94995 7

Typeset in Bembo by Hewer Text UK Ltd, Edinburgh
Printed and bound in Great Britain by Clays Ltd, Elcograf S.p.A

The paper and board used in this book
are made from wood from responsible sources.

Hodder Children's Books
An imprint of
Hachette Children's Group
Part of Hodder and Stoughton
Carmelite House
50 Victoria Embankment
London EC4Y 0DZ

An Hachette UK Company
www.hachette.co.uk

www.hachettechildrens.co.uk

*Pride and Prejudice*, by Jane Austen, was first published in 1813.

This was the Regency era — a time when English society was sharply divided by wealth and women were expected to marry young.

The heroine of this story, Elizabeth, might have some things in common with modern readers, but she lived in a very different world.

You can find out more about Jane Austen and what England was like in 1813 at the back of this book!

# MAIN CHARACTERS

**MR BENNET AND MRS BENNET**
The parents of five girls of marriageable age.
The family live at Longbourn, near the village of Meryton.

**MISS ELIZABETH BENNET**
Our heroine! Bright and bold, and determined to only ever marry for love.

**MISS KITTY BENNET**
Lively and fun-loving, likes nothing more than a good ball.

**MISS MARY BENNET**
Studious and disapproving of her younger sisters. Would rather read or play the piano than go to a ball.

**MISS JANE BENNET**
The eldest Bennet sister. Kind and generous, thinks the best of everyone.

**MISS LYDIA BENNET**
The youngest and most boisterous, longs to be married before her older sisters.

## MR GARDINER AND MRS GARDINER
Uncle and aunt to the Bennet sisters. They live in London.

## MISS CHARLOTTE LUCAS
A great friend of Elizabeth Bennet, and a similar age. Daughter of Mr and Mrs Lucas, and sister of Miss Maria Lucas, who is a little younger than the Bennet sisters.

## MR COLLINS
A distant cousin of Mr Bennet, and his only male heir. The parson of Lady Catherine de Bourgh's local church. A little bit older than the Bennet sisters.

## LADY CATHERINE DE BOURGH
A very wealthy, aristocratic woman who lives in a grand house called Rosings Park. Has one daughter, Miss Anne de Bourgh.

**MR WICKHAM**
An officer in the army regiment
stationed in the village of Meryton.

**MISS BINGLEY**
The sister of Mr Bingley, she lives mostly in
London but comes to stay in Netherfield.
She is rather haughty and looks down
on people who live in the countryside.
A similar age to the Bennet sisters.

**MR BINGLEY**
A newcomer to Meryton, he has
just moved into a large house called
Netherfield. A close friend of Mr Darcy.
A little bit older than the Bennet sisters.

**MR DARCY**
A great friend of Mr Bingley. Lives in a grand
house in Derbyshire called Pemberley. He is
the nephew of Lady Catherine de Bourgh.
A little bit older than the Bennet sisters.

**MISS GEORGIANA DARCY**
The sister of Mr Darcy – he has
taken care of her since their parents
died. Loves playing the piano. A little
younger than the Bennet sisters.

CHAPTER ONE

A long time ago, in a country house called Longbourn, there lived the Bennet family. They were Mr and Mrs Bennet and their five daughters: Jane, Elizabeth, Mary, Kitty and Lydia.

The five girls were quite different from each other. Jane, the eldest, was kind and gentle. Elizabeth, who came next, had a lively sense of humour. Mary thought herself rather studious and serious, while Kitty and Lydia, who were the youngest sisters, were always giggling and getting up to mischief.

Mr and Mrs Bennet did not have very much in common either. What Mr Bennet liked doing best was sitting by the fire in his library reading a book, whilst Mrs Bennet preferred visiting her friends to gossip about everything that was going on in the neighbourhood. But what she loved doing more than anything else was picturing the future weddings of her five daughters, and imagining the rich and important husbands she hoped they would have.

One day, she came home to Longbourn full of excitement.

'My dear Mr Bennet!' she announced. 'Have you heard? We have a new neighbour at Netherfield Park! His name is Mr Bingley, and he is a single young man with a large fortune. What a fine thing for our girls!'

'What do you mean?' asked Mr Bennet. 'How can it affect them?'

'Mr Bennet, how can you be so tiresome? You must realise that I am thinking of his marrying one of them!' exclaimed Mrs Bennet.

'Is that his plan, then, in moving to the

neighbourhood?' asked Mr Bennet, who liked to tease.

'His plan? *Nonsense*, how can you say such a thing? But you know, it is very likely that he *may* fall in love with one of them. You must visit him as soon as you can, and make friends!'

But Mr Bennet just shrugged. 'Oh, I'll just send him a note to say he can marry any of my daughters he chooses,' he said casually. 'Though of course, I'll throw in an especially good word for Lizzy.'

'You will do no such thing!' said Mrs Bennet, horrified by this suggestion. 'Anyway, Lizzy is no better than any of the others, though you favour her the most.'

'They're all silly enough – but Lizzy has more quickness than her sisters,' said Mr Bennet mischievously.

'Mr Bennet, how can you be so rude about your own children? You take delight in vexing me!' exclaimed Mrs Bennet. 'You have no sympathy for my poor nerves!'

'That's not true,' protested Mr Bennet at once. 'I am very fond of your nerves – they are old friends of mine. I have heard you talking about them for the last twenty years!'

As a matter of fact, Mr Bennet had every intention of going to see Mr Bingley. He was one of the

first of the neighbours to pay him a visit – although he didn't say a word about it to the rest of the family.

Instead, when he saw Elizabeth trimming a new bonnet, he said, 'I hope Mr Bingley will like it.'

'None of us have any idea what Mr Bingley might like, since you will not visit him!' said Mrs Bennet, crossly. She turned to Kitty, in a temper.

'Don't keep coughing, Kitty! Have a little compassion on my nerves.'

But Mr Bennet did not seem to notice his wife's bad mood. He went on making remarks about Mr Bingley, until at last Mrs Bennet cried out, 'I am *sick* of Mr Bingley!'

Only then did Mr Bennet say, 'I am sorry to hear that. If I had known this morning, I wouldn't have gone to visit him. It is very unlucky – well, I suppose we can't escape making friends with him now.'

All at once, Mrs Bennet's temper was swept away by a tide of delight. 'My dear Mr Bennet! How pleased I am that you have visited him. And what a good joke too, that you never said a word about it!'

'Well, Kitty, I think you may cough as much as you like now,' observed Mr Bennet with a grin.

# CHAPTER TWO

Mrs Bennet wasn't the only one who was excited about the arrival of Mr Bingley. Everyone in the neighbourhood was talking about him, especially because it was a truth universally acknowledged that a single man in possession of a good fortune must be in want of a wife.

Elizabeth and her sisters soon learned that he was young and handsome, rode a black horse and wore a blue coat. Best of all, he was fond of dancing – and he was going to attend the very next ball.

A whisper ran through the room when Mr Bingley arrived in the ballroom. He was just as young, handsome and jolly-looking as everyone had said. What was more, he was not alone, he was accompanied by two ladies and two gentlemen. They were his sister Mrs Hurst and her husband Mr Hurst; his unmarried sister, Miss Bingley; and his very good friend, Mr Darcy.

Everyone turned to admire the newcomers. Mrs Hurst and Miss Bingley were elegant ladies

dressed in the very latest London fashions. As for Mr Darcy, a rumour rushed around the room that he was even richer than Mr Bingley, with a big house in Derbyshire and a very large fortune. All the ladies agreed at once that he was the most handsome man they had ever seen.

But Mr Darcy was not popular for long. While Mr Bingley chatted, danced and made friends with everyone, Mr Darcy stood all by himself, looking haughty and aloof.

Elizabeth, who was sitting watching the dancing, noticed Mr Bingley come bustling over to him.

'Come, Darcy,' he said cheerfully. 'You must dance. I hate to see you standing about by yourself like this.'

'I certainly shall not,' drawled Mr Darcy. 'You know I hate it. Besides, your sisters are already dancing, and I couldn't possibly dance with anyone else here.'

Mr Bingley shook his head at his friend in surprise. 'But the girls here are so pleasant – and several of them are very pretty!'

'*You* have been dancing with the only handsome girl in the room,' said Mr Darcy, glancing over at Elizabeth's sister Jane.

Mr Bingley's cheeks turned bright pink. 'I think

she is the most beautiful creature I've ever seen,' he confessed. 'But look, Darcy – there is one of her sisters. She is very pretty too and I'm sure very agreeable.'

Mr Darcy looked round to where Elizabeth was sitting by herself. 'Hmmm. She is tolerable I suppose, but not handsome enough to tempt *me*. Besides, I am in no mood to dance with a young lady who is ignored by other men.'

At first, Elizabeth felt rather offended by this. But then she thought how pompous and silly Mr Darcy sounded, and what a funny story it would make to tell her friends. Soon she was giggling over it with her friend Charlotte Lucas.

She didn't notice Mr Darcy glance in her direction – for the first time looking a little uncomfortable.

The Bennets went home from the ball in high spirits. Mrs Bennet was overjoyed that Mr Bingley had taken a liking to Jane; Mary was proud because her piano-playing had been praised; and Kitty and Lydia were very excited that Mr Bingley had promised to soon host a ball of his own at Netherfield Park.

Back at Longbourn, they found Mr Bennet reading by the fire.

'We have had a most delightful evening,' began Mrs Bennet. 'Jane was so admired by Mr Bingley! Of course, he danced with Charlotte Lucas first, which vexed me greatly. But then he danced with Jane twice, and then with Lizzy – and what do you think he did next?'

'Enough of his partners,' groaned Mr Bennet. 'I wish he had sprained his ankle in the first dance.'

Mrs Bennet paid him no attention. 'But his friend, Mr Darcy – *what* a proud and horrid man! He refused to dance with Lizzy, you know. Next time, you shouldn't dance with him even if he *does* ask you,' she instructed Elizabeth.

Elizabeth laughed. 'I think I can safely promise you never to dance with Mr Darcy.'

But Mrs Bennet had already begun talking about Mr Bingley's sisters. 'Such charming women. I never saw such elegant dresses! The lace on Mrs Hurst's gown—'

But the lace on Mrs Hurst's gown was too much for Mr Bennet. He hurried away to the library to escape his wife's chatter, as fast as he could go.

# CHAPTER THREE

The next day, Jane and Elizabeth, who always discussed everything together, had a long talk about Mr Bingley.

'He's everything a young man should be,' sighed Jane dreamily. 'He's good-natured and sensible, lively and cheerful.'

'And handsome, which a young man ought to be if he possibly can,' said Elizabeth with a grin. 'I give you permission to like him. You've liked stupider people before.'

Jane laughed, but Elizabeth went on, 'You're much too ready to like people in general, you know. You never see a fault in anyone – I've never heard you say anything mean about anybody in your life! What about Mr Bingley's sisters, for example? They certainly aren't much like him.'

'Perhaps not at first, but once I talked to them for a while, I liked them very much,' said Jane, smiling happily. 'I think they will be charming neighbours.'

But Elizabeth wasn't so sure. Whilst Mr Bingley had been easy and friendly, his sisters had seemed proud and haughty – rather like Mr Darcy.

The more Jane and Mr Bingley got to know each other, the more they liked each other. Mrs Bennet was overjoyed, and spent hours imagining what a wonderful wedding they would have. But Elizabeth thought it was a bit too soon for that.

'She's only known him for a fortnight!' she said to Charlotte, when they were together at a party at Charlotte's house, Lucas Lodge. 'She's danced with him a few times, but she doesn't really know him yet.'

'Well, I think she's got as good a chance of being happy with him as with anyone.' Charlotte shrugged, in her usual down-to-earth way. 'You've got to be practical about it, you know. Marriage is really about security – happiness is just a matter of luck.'

Elizabeth didn't agree – but before she could say anything else, they were interrupted by Lydia, who came barging past them to the piano, where Mary was playing a dull and difficult concerto.

'Mary! Play a jig so we can dance!' she demanded.

Mary pulled a sour face but, with a sigh, she did as she was asked and all around the room, people began finding partners to join the dance.

Charlotte's father, Sir William Lucas, nodded his head in time to the cheerful music. 'What a marvellous amusement dancing is!' he observed heartily to Mr Darcy, who was standing by himself, silent as usual. 'And your friend dances so well,' he observed, looking over to where Mr Bingley was once again dancing with Jane. 'I'm sure you do too, of course.'

At that moment, he caught sight of Elizabeth. 'My dear Miss Eliza – why aren't you dancing? Mr Darcy, allow me to present this young lady to you as a wonderful dancing partner.'

Elizabeth felt very embarrassed. She was certain Mr Darcy was going to make another rude remark – so before he had chance to speak, she said hurriedly that she wasn't planning to dance. But to her surprise, Mr Darcy said rather stiffly, 'I would be honoured if you would dance with me, Miss Elizabeth.'

For a moment, Elizabeth didn't know what to say – but she had no intention of dancing with Mr Darcy, so she quickly excused herself and hurried away.

A minute later, Miss Bingley came sweeping over in her expensive gown to where Mr Darcy was standing. 'I can guess what you're thinking,' she said, glancing around her with contempt. 'How *awful* it would be to spend many in evenings in such tedious company as this!'

'Actually, I was thinking of something more pleasant,' said Mr Darcy. 'I was thinking what fine eyes Miss Elizabeth Bennet has.'

'Miss Elizabeth Bennet?' Miss Bingley goggled. 'I am all astonishment!' She laughed her high, rather silly laugh – but anyone looking at her closely would have noticed that she didn't really look amused, but instead very cross indeed.

# CHAPTER FOUR

The next day, Kitty and Lydia came home bubbling over with news. A regiment of soldiers had arrived in the nearby village of Meryton and was to stay there all winter. The two girls were full of excitement about the handsome officers in their smart red coats, and they could talk of nothing else.

'I've suspected it for some time, but now I know for sure,' said Mr Bennet with a heavy sigh. 'You are two of the silliest girls in the country!'

But Mrs Bennet didn't think their interest in the officers was silly at all. 'I wouldn't mind if a smart young colonel wanted to marry one of my daughters,' she said, adding wistfully, 'You know, when I was a girl, I liked a redcoat myself once . . .'

Just then, a footman arrived with a note for Jane. It was from Miss Bingley, inviting Jane to dine at Netherfield Park with herself and Mrs Hurst, while Mr Bingley and the other gentlemen dined out with the officers.

'May I have the carriage?' Jane asked eagerly.

'No!' insisted Mrs Bennet at once. 'You must go on horseback. It looks like rain – and if so, they will ask you to stay the night. That way you won't miss the chance to see Mr Bingley.'

Sure enough, not long after Jane had set out, it began to rain very hard. 'What a good idea of mine,' said Mrs Bennet, as pleased as if she had made it rain herself.

But at breakfast the next morning, a note arrived from Netherfield for Elizabeth:

*Dear Lizzy,*

*I am very unwell this morning. I got wet through yesterday on my ride to Netherfield and now I have a cold. My friends will not hear of me returning home until I am better and insist on sending for the doctor. But don't worry – apart from a headache and a sore throat there is nothing much wrong with me.*

*Jane*

'Well, Mrs Bennet,' said Mr Bennet, after Elizabeth had read this aloud. 'If Jane should die from this illness, at least you will know it was all for Mr Bingley's sake.'

'Don't be silly. People don't die of little trifling colds!' protested Mrs Bennet.

But just the same, Elizabeth felt worried about Jane, and made up her mind to walk over to Netherfield to see her.

Mrs Bennet did not like this idea one bit. 'You

can't possibly walk in all this dirt. You won't be fit to be seen when you get there!'

'I shall be fit to see Jane, which is all I want,' said Elizabeth stoutly. 'It's only three miles after all.'

It did not take Elizabeth long to cross the fields to Netherfield. She loved walking and being outdoors; it was a pleasant day now the rain had stopped and she walked briskly, jumping over stiles and springing over puddles. By the time she arrived at Mr Bingley's grand house, she had dirty stockings but a face glowing with warmth.

Everyone was surprised to see her. Mrs Hurst and Miss Bingley could hardly believe she had walked so far. Whilst Mr Bingley welcomed her warmly, Mr Darcy said little, and Mr Hurst nothing at all – because he was only interested in his breakfast.

While Elizabeth went to see Jane, who was resting in a guest bedroom, down in the drawing room, Miss Bingley and Mrs Hurst were already gossiping about her:

'Really, she looked almost *wild*!'

'What was she thinking, scampering about the country, just because her sister has a cold? Walking three miles in the mud and dirt by herself?'

'Her hair was so untidy.'

'And her petticoat was six inches deep in mud – I am certain of it.'

'I thought it was very kind of Miss Elizabeth to come all this way to see her sister,' said Mr Bingley indignantly. 'I didn't even notice her petticoat.'

'You noticed it, I am sure, Mr Darcy,' said Miss Bingley slyly. 'I'm afraid this may affect your admiration of her *fine eyes*.'

But Mr Darcy only shrugged. 'Actually, they were brightened by the exercise,' was all he said.

Jane was feeling very ill, so Elizabeth was relieved when Mr Bingley insisted she stay on at Netherfield to look after her sister – sending a servant back to Longbourn to collect some clothes for her.

That evening, when Jane had fallen asleep, Elizabeth came down to the drawing room. Mr Bingley invited her to join in the card game they were playing, but she said she would read a book instead.

Mr Hurst stared at her in astonishment. 'You prefer *reading* to cards?' he asked.

'Miss Bennet despises cards,' announced Miss Bingley. 'She is a great reader and enjoys nothing else.'

Elizabeth raised her eyebrows. 'Actually, I enjoy lots of things,' she replied honestly.

Miss Bingley only laughed her silly laugh.

Soon, the card game was finished. Mr Darcy picked up a book too, but Miss Bingley turned to Elizabeth. 'Miss Eliza, why don't you join me to take a stroll around the room? It is so refreshing.'

Miss Bingley tucked her arm through Elizabeth's

as though they were the best of friends, and began
to parade up and down the room with her. When
Mr Darcy glanced up from his book as they passed,
Miss Bingley invited him to join them too.

'But surely that would destroy the point,' he replied.

'Whatever do you mean?' said Miss Bingley, with a laugh.

'Well, you are either sharing secrets with each other – in which case you wouldn't want *me* listening. Or perhaps you want me to admire you as you walk, which I can do much better sitting here by the fire.'

'What a shocking thing to say!' cried Miss Bingley, pretending to be outraged. 'Miss Eliza – how shall we punish him for it?'

'That's easy,' said Elizabeth at once. 'Tease him for making such a suggestion – laugh at him.'

'Nobody could possibly *tease* or *laugh at* Mr Darcy,' said Miss Bingley very seriously.

'Couldn't they?' asked Elizabeth, lifting her eyebrows. 'That's a shame – I love to laugh.'

'But there would be nothing to laugh at. Mr Darcy has no flaws!'

'Of course I do – just the same as anyone else,'

said Mr Darcy stiffly. 'Though I must admit, I *do* try to avoid any weaknesses which are easily laughed at, or seem ridiculous,' he added.

'Such as pride, perhaps?' suggested Elizabeth in an innocent voice.

'I don't think pride is a weakness,' said Mr Darcy – and Elizabeth had to turn away to hide her smile. 'But I do have plenty of shortcomings. I have a hot temper, and I find it hard to forgive people. My good opinion, once lost, is lost for ever.'

'That *is* a weakness,' agreed Elizabeth. 'But I can't laugh at it.'

'I think it's time for some music,' said Miss Bingley, hurrying to the piano – not much liking this conversation in which she didn't seem to be playing any part.

The next morning, Mrs Bennet arrived at Netherfield to see how Jane was getting on, bringing Kitty and Lydia with her. She was pleased to find that Jane seemed a little better – but she was not going to let Mr Bingley know that. She wanted Jane to stay at Netherfield for as long as she could!

'She is much too ill to be moved,' she said, shaking her head mournfully. 'We must take advantage of your kindness for a little longer.'

'Moved? It must not be thought of!' exclaimed Mr Bingley at once.

'She will receive every possible attention,' said Miss Bingley, coldly polite.

Mrs Bennet was quick to admire everything at Netherfield. 'You must be so comfortable here, you would never think of going back to London.'

'When I am in the country I never wish to go to London,' Mr Bingley agreed. 'Though I must admit, when I am in town it is just the same. I am very happy in both places.'

'But country society is rather confined and

unvarying,' observed Mr Darcy.

'*Confined? Unvarying?*' exclaimed Mrs Bennet, much offended. 'I'll have you know, we dine with *twenty-four* families,' she said, thinking this a very large and impressive number.

Mr Bingley nodded politely, but Mrs Hurst sniggered, and Miss Bingley gave Mr Darcy a little smirk. Elizabeth hurried to change the subject. 'Has Charlotte Lucas been to visit?' she asked her mother.

'She called yesterday with her father,' replied Mrs Bennet, still rather cross. 'What an agreeable man Sir William is. That is *my* idea of a true gentleman,' she said, giving Mr Darcy a glower. 'And Charlotte Lucas is a very good sort of girl, though she is rather plain. What a shame she's not as beautiful as Jane,' she added, with a sidelong look at Mr Bingley.

All this time, Kitty and Lydia had been whispering to one another. Now Lydia spoke up boldly. 'Mr Bingley, didn't you say you'd give a ball at Netherfield? It would be shameful if you didn't keep your promise.'

'Of course I will,' said Mr Bingley cheerfully. 'When your sister is better, you may name the day of the ball.'

Mrs Bennet and her daughters were delighted. Soon afterwards they left, and Elizabeth returned to Jane's room – leaving Miss Bingley and Mrs Hurst to pick over their visit, and to criticise the behaviour of the Bennet family.

But however hard they tried, they could not persuade Mr Darcy to say anything rude about Elizabeth – in spite of all Miss Bingley's jokes about *fine eyes*.

# CHAPTER FIVE

Elizabeth was relieved when Jane was well enough to go home. Although she liked Mr Bingley more than ever, she hadn't much enjoyed the company of his haughty sisters. Back at Longbourn she found everything was just as usual: Mrs Bennet wanted to relate all the local gossip, and Kitty and Lydia were full of tales about the officers, whilst Mary pursed her lips disapprovingly. But it was Mr Bennet who had the most interesting news of all.

'I hope you have ordered a good dinner today,' he began, at breakfast-time. 'Because we have a visitor coming – a gentleman.'

Mrs Bennet's eyes sparkled and she looked over at Jane. 'Oh! It is Mr Bingley, I am sure!'

'It is not Mr Bingley. It is a stranger – someone I've never met before,' said Mr Bennet, relishing the drama of his announcement. 'I have received a letter from my distant cousin, Mr Collins – who when I am dead, could turn you all out of this house as soon as he pleases.'

'Oh! I cannot bear to hear that mentioned! Do not speak of that odious man!' cried Mrs Bennet at once.

Jane and Elizabeth exchanged glances. They knew exactly what she meant. When Mr Bennet died, Longbourn and all his property would not be passed on to his wife or daughters. Instead, they would be inherited by his closest male relative – his unknown cousin, Mr Collins – leaving his wife and any unmarried daughters without a home. Mrs Bennet thought this very cruel, and Elizabeth and Jane couldn't help agreeing that it did not seem very fair.

'Listen to his letter,' said Mr Bennet.

Dear Sir,

The disagreement between you and my late father always made me very uneasy. Since I have had the misfortune to lose him, I have longed to <u>repair the breach</u>. I have recently become a parson, and been fortunate enough to be appointed to the parish of the <u>Right Honourable Lady Catherine de Bourgh</u> – and in my profession, I feel it is my duty to promote <u>peace in all families</u>.

I hope this letter will be well-received, and the fact that I am next in line to inherit Longbourn will not lead you to reject my offer of an <u>olive branch</u>. I should hate to be the means of causing any future difficulties for your <u>delightful daughters</u>, and am ready to make them <u>every possible amend</u>.

If you have no objection, I shall visit you on Monday 18th November, arriving by four o'clock.

I remain, dear sir, with compliments to your lady and daughters, <u>your well-wisher and friend</u>,

William Collins

'He sounds rather pompous,' remarked Elizabeth.

'Doesn't he?' said her father, grinning. 'I think his visit is going to be most entertaining.'

Mr Collins arrived at Longbourn at four o'clock, just as his letter had said. He was an earnest, red-faced young man who spoke in a very flowery manner, paying lavish compliments on everything from the furniture, to the dinner, to the beauty of the five Bennet sisters.

He was even more gushing about his work as a parson and his grand patron, Lady Catherine de Bourgh. Not only did she invite him to dine at her magnificent house, Rosings Park, she praised the sermons he gave in church, and had even paid a visit to his humble parsonage with her daughter, Miss Anne de Bourgh, he told them.

'Miss de Bourgh has unfortunately been unwell,' went on Mr Collins, who by now had been talking for some time. 'Her health has prevented her going to town. I told Lady Catherine that London society has been deprived of its brightest ornament! You see, I am always happy to offer delicate little compliments that are pleasing to ladies,' he noted to Mr Bennet, looking very satisfied with himself.

'How lucky that you have such a talent for it,' said Mr Bennet, hiding a smile. 'Tell me, do you come up with these remarks on the spur of the moment – or do you plan them in advance?'

'Well, I must admit I do sometimes amuse myself by arranging a few elegant compliments, which may be adapted for different occasions,' said Mr Collins smugly.

He certainly had plenty of 'elegant compliments' to pay the Bennet sisters. He revealed that Lady Catherine had advised him to marry soon, and Elizabeth began to suspect that he had come to Longbourn looking for a wife.

When he wasn't complimenting the sisters, Mr Collins spent much of his time with Mr Bennet, following him into his library, supposedly to look at his books, but in fact, to talk even more about Lady Catherine. It didn't take Mr Bennet very long to suggest that perhaps Mr Collins might like to get some fresh air and accompany his daughters on a walk into Meryton instead.

Mr Collins filled most of the walk with pompous nothings. Jane, Elizabeth and Mary did their best to listen politely, but Lydia and Kitty paid him very little attention. They were excited by the prospect of seeing the army officers, and not even a smart bonnet in a shop window could possibly distract them from that.

'Good morning, Mr Denny!' they called out, very pleased to see one of their particular friends amongst the officers when they reached Meryton. They were even more pleased when they saw that he was accompanied by a stranger – a handsome and dashing-looking young fellow who had them both in a flutter of excitement at once. Mr Denny introduced him to everyone as Mr Wickham, who was soon to join the regiment.

'Hooray!' whispered Lydia to Kitty. 'He only needs a uniform to make him *completely* charming.'

As they stood talking, the sound of hooves was heard in the street – and presently Mr Darcy and Mr Bingley appeared on their tall, glossy horses. Mr Bingley came over at once to speak to Jane.

'We were on our way to Longbourn to ask after your health,' he said heartily, delighted to see that Jane was better.

But while Jane chatted with Mr Bingley, Elizabeth noticed to her surprise that Mr Darcy was staring at Mr Wickham – and that Mr Wickham was staring back at him. Mr Darcy's face had turned rather white, Mr Wickham's rather pink. After a few moments, Mr Wickham touched his hat to Mr Darcy, and Mr Darcy nodded coldly in return. *What could it mean?* Elizabeth wondered with great interest.

After a few moments, Mr Bingley said goodbye and went on with Mr Darcy, and the two officers also said their farewells. Kitty and Lydia nudged each other in excitement, so delighted by Mr Wickham that they declared all the other officers were 'stupid and disagreeable fellows' in comparison. But although she too thought him very handsome and charming, Elizabeth was more intrigued by his strange interaction with Mr Darcy.

# CHAPTER SIX

The very next evening the Bennet sisters set out for Meryton, where they were to attend a supper party hosted by their aunt, Mrs Phillips. They were joined by Mr Collins, who was full of lavish compliments for Mrs Phillips and her home. In fact, he admired her drawing room so much that he loudly declared it reminded him of a small summer breakfast room at Rosings Park – the home of Lady Catherine de Bourgh herself. At first Mrs Phillips looked rather put out at this comparison, but when she had heard Mr Collins's long explanation of how grand Lady Catherine was, and had been informed that the chimney-piece in Her Ladyship's drawing room had cost eight hundred pounds, she cheered up quite a bit.

Meanwhile, Lydia and Kitty were delighted to see that lots of officers were in attendance – including the new arrival, the charming Mr Wickham. Elizabeth was pleased when he came to sit beside her, and began a lively conversation. She wished she dared ask him about his strange encounter with Mr Darcy – so she was pleased

when Mr Wickham brought up the subject himself.

'How long has Mr Darcy been staying at Netherfield?' he began.

'About a month,' said Elizabeth. Wanting him to say more, she added, 'He has a large house in Derbyshire, I believe.'

'That's right,' said Mr Wickham. 'It is called Pemberley. I know it well – in fact, I grew up there. Mr Darcy and I spent our childhood together. You'll probably be surprised to hear that, when you saw how coldly he greeted me yesterday. Tell me . . . do you know Mr Darcy well?'

'As much as I wish to!' admitted Elizabeth boldly. 'I spent four days in the same house as him, and I found him very disagreeable.'

'Not many people would agree with you,' said Mr Wickham with a sigh.

'Really?' asked Elizabeth in surprise. 'He is not at all well-liked here. Everyone is disgusted with his pride.'

'I can't say I'm sorry to hear it. Usually people are impressed by his money and his imposing manners.'

'I hope him being here won't affect your plans to stay in the neighbourhood?'

'Oh no, I wouldn't allow myself to be scared off by Mr Darcy,' said Mr Wickham, with a cheerful grin. 'We are not on friendly terms, but I have no reason to avoid him. But seeing him does make me feel regretful.' He looked more serious for a moment, and explained, 'His father, the late Mr Darcy, was my godfather, and the best friend I ever had. My father was his steward, you know. He planned that I should one day go into the church – it's all I ever wanted. But when his father died, Mr Darcy ignored his wishes, and denied me the job and money that he had arranged for me. So I had to give up my dream of becoming a parson – and now I must make my own way in the world.'

'How dreadful!' exclaimed Elizabeth, shocked

that anyone could be so unkind. 'How could Mr Darcy do such a thing?'

'He claimed I wasn't suited for the church.' Mr Wickham sighed again. 'I must admit, I do have a temper and perhaps sometimes I speak more freely than I should. But the truth is, Mr Darcy dislikes me. He was jealous of my close relationship with his father.'

'I hadn't thought Mr Darcy as bad as that,' said Elizabeth, shaking her head – but then she recalled their conversation at Netherfield, and how he had boasted about being unforgiving. 'It makes me even more surprised that he is such a good friend of Mr Bingley, who is so kind and good-natured. He mustn't have any idea what Mr Darcy is really like.'

Just then, Mrs Phillips and Mr Collins came to sit down at a table beside them. Mr Collins was still talking away about Lady Catherine, and Mrs Phillips was listening attentively. Mr Wickham gave a sudden smile: 'Did you know that Lady

Catherine de Bourgh is Mr Darcy's aunt?' he asked Elizabeth. 'They are very alike – just as proud and rude as each other!'

'No I didn't,' Elizabeth said with a laugh. 'I had never even heard of Lady Catherine de Bourgh until Mr Collins arrived – but he talks of little else.'

'Her daughter, Miss Anne de Bourgh, is set to marry Mr Darcy,' added Mr Wickham.

Elizabeth smiled to herself, thinking of poor Miss Bingley and her efforts to get Mr Darcy's attention. They would all be for nothing if he was to marry Lady Catherine's rich daughter.

But there was no more time for her to talk with Mr Wickham, for the supper party had come to an end. Soon the Bennets were on their way home in their carriage: Kitty and Lydia full of chatter about the evening with the officers, whilst Mr Collins described in great detail each and every dish he had eaten at supper. Elizabeth put up with the babble impatiently, eager to be alone with Jane so she could tell her all she had learned from her conversation with Mr Wickham.

When they were at last by themselves, and Elizabeth poured out the tale, Jane's eyes were round with astonishment. 'But there must be some mistake!' she exclaimed. 'Surely Mr Darcy could never have ignored his father's wishes in that way – whatever he thinks of Mr Wickham.'

'I think it's far more likely he would do so than that Mr Wickham would make up such a story,' insisted Elizabeth, her eyes flashing with indignation. 'Besides – he told me all the details, names and facts. He was so frank and honest.'

'How horrid – and distressing,' said Jane unhappily. 'And Mr Darcy is such a good friend of Mr Bingley's too. Oh, one doesn't know *what* to think about it!'

'I beg your pardon,' said Elizabeth decidedly. 'One knows *exactly* what to think.'

# CHAPTER SEVEN

Longbourn was a flurry of excitement as the day of Mr Bingley's ball at Netherfield approached. There were ballgowns to choose, bonnets to trim and all manner of important preparations to be made.

Everyone was looking forward to the ball: Lydia and Kitty loved nothing so much as a party; Jane was eager to spend another evening in the company of Mr Bingley; and as for Elizabeth, she was secretly looking forward to seeing Mr Wickham again, and to have chance to dance with him. Even Mary, who did not usually share her sisters' enthusiasm for balls, said she was looking forward to what she called 'an evening of recreation and amusement'.

'But do you think it would be proper for a parson to attend?' Elizabeth asked Mr Collins – hoping that he might decide to stay behind at Longbourn.

But Mr Collins declared he was quite certain that even Lady Catherine herself could not possibly disapprove of him coming with them to Netherfield. 'Not for a ball of this kind, given by a young man of character, to respectable people,' he declared primly, adding, 'I hope to have the honour of dancing with all my fair cousins over the course of the evening – and I should like you, Miss Elizabeth, to be my partner in the first two dances.'

Elizabeth's heart sank. She'd been hoping to dance those dances with Mr Wickham – and now she would have to be partners with Mr Collins instead.

But there was more disappointment in store. When the Bennets arrived at Netherfield, and were shown into the grand drawing room, Mr Wickham was nowhere to be seen amongst the officers in their scarlet coats.

Mr Denny hurried over to greet them, and to explain that Mr Wickham would not be attending the ball, as he had been called away on business. He whispered to Elizabeth, 'Though I don't think he would have been called away just now if he hadn't wished to avoid a *certain gentleman* here tonight.'

Elizabeth felt downcast – but she was rarely in a bad mood for long, and she was soon consoling herself by entertaining her friend Charlotte with tales of all the peculiarities of Mr Collins.

All too soon it was time for the first dances, which Elizabeth did not enjoy in the least. Mr Collins was a dreadful dancer: he got all the steps wrong, trampled on her feet, turned in the wrong direction and bumped into people, apologising all the while. Her cheeks burned bright red with embarrassment and she was relieved when the dances were over and she could escape from Mr Collins again.

But before she could return to Charlotte, Mr Darcy suddenly appeared at her side. 'Miss Elizabeth, would you care to dance?' he asked.

Elizabeth was so surprised that she agreed almost without realising what she had done. As soon as the words were out of her mouth, she wished she could take them back. As if Mr Collins wasn't bad enough – now she would have to dance with Mr Darcy too!

They stood awkwardly together waiting for the music to start. For the first few minutes of the dance, neither of them said anything. Elizabeth concentrated on the steps, wondering if they would be silent for the whole dance. After a while, she felt she had to make a polite remark – but when Mr Darcy did not even bother to reply, she began to feel cross.

'It is *your* turn to speak now,' she said sternly.

'My turn?'

'Well, we have to say *something*. It would look odd to be silent for the whole dance – even if we are both unsociable people.'

Mr Darcy looked surprised. 'I'm sure that's not true of you,' he said.

Another silence fell, until at last he asked stiffly, 'Do you and your sisters walk often into Meryton?'

'Quite often. When you met us there the other morning, we had been making a new friend – Mr Wickham,' said Elizabeth, wanting to see how he would react.

The effect was immediate. Mr Darcy looked haughtier than ever. 'Mr Wickham is good at making friends wherever he goes,' he declared disdainfully. 'Whether he is good at keeping them is not so certain.'

'He has been unlucky enough to lose your friendship,' replied Elizabeth shortly. 'And in a way that he will suffer from all his life.'

Mr Darcy looked annoyed, but just then, the dance came to an end, and Sir William Lucas appeared, rubbing his hands together with delight. 'Such superior dancing!' he said appreciatively. 'I hope to have the pleasure of seeing you dancing together often – especially when a certain *event* takes place, eh, Miss Eliza?' He gave Elizabeth a quick wink and nodded towards Jane and Mr

Bingley. 'What a wonderful occasion that will be!'

But Mr Darcy did not seem to think the idea very wonderful at all. Instead he frowned and looked sharply over at Jane and Mr Bingley, before excusing himself abruptly.

No sooner had Mr Darcy and Sir William left her than Elizabeth saw Miss Bingley sweeping towards her. She wore feathered plumes on her head, and a disdainful smile on her face.

'So, Miss Eliza,' she began. 'I hear you are quite delighted with Mr Wickham.' She gave a little giggle. 'I wonder if you know he is no more than the son of old Mr Darcy's steward? You mustn't listen to everything he says, you know. His stories about Mr Darcy are all false. Mr Darcy has always been terribly good to him, in spite of the fact that Mr Wickham treated him quite dreadfully! I don't know any of the details – but I do know Mr Darcy wasn't in the least to blame.' She smiled in a self-satisfied manner. 'Oh, *poor* Miss Eliza, I'm sorry to be the bearer of bad news about your favourite. Although really, considering his low birth, I suppose you couldn't expect much more.'

Elizabeth felt a hot burst of temper. 'I don't see that there's anything wrong with being the son of Mr Darcy's steward!' she exclaimed. 'Mr Wickham told me that himself.'

Miss Bingley gave another twittering laugh, 'I beg your pardon,' she said, turning away. 'Excuse my interference. It was kindly meant.'

Miss Bingley swept off again, as Mr Collins came bouncing up with a beaming smile upon his red face. 'I have just made a wonderful discovery,' he announced. 'Here at the ball is the nephew of none other than Lady Catherine de Bourgh! I am so thankful I discovered it in time to pay my respects.'

'Do you mean to say that you are going to speak to Mr Darcy?' asked Elizabeth in alarm. Without a formal introduction, this would not be at all in keeping with the rules of etiquette.

'Indeed I am,' said Mr Collins, looking delighted at the prospect. 'I will be able to inform him that Her Ladyship was quite well last Thursday.'

'I'm not sure that's a very good idea,' said Elizabeth hastily – but Mr Collins only patted her on the arm. 'My dear Miss Elizabeth, I have the highest opinion in the world of you. But you must see that *I* am more fitted by my education and experience to know what is right than a young lady like yourself.'

Elizabeth felt her cheeks growing hot all over again as Mr Collins made a beeline for Mr Darcy. She could not hear exactly what he said, but she caught the words 'Rosings Park' and 'Lady Catherine de Bourgh', and she saw Mr Darcy frowning down at him, his expression a mixture of bemusement and contempt.

Mr Collins did not seem to have noticed anything was amiss. 'You see? Mr Darcy was pleased by my attentions!' he reported when he returned, puffed up with importance.

Mr Collins was not the only member of the family behaving badly. Mrs Bennet was so delighted with the idea that Jane might soon be engaged to Mr Bingley that she talked of nothing else all night long. 'And so fortunate for the other girls!' Elizabeth heard her declare loudly to Charlotte's mother, Lady Lucas. 'It will throw them into the paths of other rich men!'

Mr Darcy was looking over at Mrs Bennet in disgust. '*Shhh*!' Elizabeth whispered desperately – but her mother paid no attention.

Meanwhile, Lydia and Kitty were romping in the ballroom; at the piano, Mary was singing in a loud and tuneless voice; and Mr Collins was holding forth in another of his endless speeches. It seemed to Elizabeth that the whole family couldn't have been more embarrassing if they had tried. Thankfully Mr Bingley was so busy talking to Jane that he didn't seem to have noticed – but she knew that the sharp eyes of Mr Darcy, Miss Bingley and Mrs Hurst had seen everything.

At long last, the evening came to an end. As they travelled home in the carriage, all was quiet for once. Even Lydia was too exhausted by dancing to do more than say with a yawn, 'How tired I am!'

Jane was happily thinking of Mr Bingley, whilst beside her, Mrs Bennet dreamed of the magnificent wedding Jane would soon have, and all her expensive wedding clothes. Opposite them, feeling much less cheerful, Elizabeth was thinking over the humiliating evening that had passed – and especially that dreadful dance with Mr Darcy.

She was so busy with her thoughts that she did not notice that Mr Collins was watching her. For once, he was not talking about Lady Catherine, for he was thinking hard too – and in fact, he had just made a most important decision.

# CHAPTER EIGHT

The next morning, Mr Collins wasted no time in finding Mrs Bennet to request 'the honour of a private audience with your fair daughter, Elizabeth'. Mrs Bennet was delighted. She guessed at once what Mr Collins had in mind – and congratulated herself that she would soon have *two* daughters engaged.

'Of course!' she agreed with a beaming smile, gathering her sewing together in a great hurry and hustling Kitty out of the room. 'Come, Kitty – I want you upstairs.'

With a sudden flash of horror, Elizabeth realised what was coming. 'Don't go, Mama – Mr Collins must excuse me – he can have nothing to say to me that you and Kitty couldn't hear,' she said at once.

'Nonsense, Lizzy! Stay where you are!' Seeing that Elizabeth looked like she was about to make a dash for it out of the room, Mrs Bennet insisted, 'You *must* stay and listen to Mr Collins.'

As soon as Mrs Bennet and Kitty were gone, Mr Collins sat beside her and began to speak in his most flowery voice.

'You can hardly doubt the reason I wish to speak with you, Miss Elizabeth. From the moment I entered this house, I singled you out as the companion for my future life.

'But before I am carried away by my feelings, I will tell you my reasons for marrying,' Mr Collins went on, quite as though he was delivering a sermon. 'First, I think it is right for a clergyman to *set the example* of marriage. Secondly, I think it will add *greatly* to my happiness. And thirdly – which I probably should have mentioned first – it is the *special wish* of Lady Catherine de Bourgh. She has several times been kind enough to give me her opinion on the subject. It was the very Saturday before last, while Mrs Jenkinson was arranging Miss de Bourgh's footstool, that she said, "Mr Collins, you *must* marry. Choose an active, useful sort of person, not brought up too high."' He beamed at Elizabeth as though paying her a great compliment. 'Of course, when you are my wife, you too will have the pleasure of Her Ladyship's company. I think she will appreciate your liveliness – especially when moderated by the respect that must of course be paid to a lady of such importance!'

Elizabeth listened in horror as, seemingly without pausing for breath, Mr Collins went on. 'As to my particular choice – since I am to inherit Longbourn after the death of your father, I made up my mind that it would be the right thing to do to choose a wife from amongst his daughters. So now nothing else remains but for me to assure you of my feelings for you. It does not matter to me that you have no fortune – I do not care at all for such things. I shall never complain about it when *we are married*!'

Elizabeth had to interrupt him before he could say any more. She could not bear it: the thought of being married to Mr Collins was simply too awful. 'You are too hasty!' she cried. 'I haven't answered you yet! Thank you for your proposal – but I'm afraid I must decline.'

But Mr Collins was not put off so easily. 'I have heard that it is usual for young ladies to reject the man who they secretly plan to accept when he first proposes,' he said with a little chuckle. 'I am not discouraged in the slightest.'

'I'm serious!' protested Elizabeth. 'You could not make me happy and I am the last person in the world who could make *you* happy either.'

'But I will make a very worthy husband. Think of my situation in life – and my connections with the noble family of de Bourgh,' declared Mr Collins, a little huffy now. 'And you must remember, my dear cousin, it is quite likely no one else will ever propose to you. When I speak to you about this again, I will hope to receive a more favourable answer.'

Elizabeth stared. Was there anything she could do or say to make Mr Collins understand that she would never agree to marry him? 'Thank you again for your proposal but to accept is impossible,' she stated as clearly as she could. 'I wish you every happiness, but I cannot marry you.'

'You cannot possibly be serious in turning me down,' Mr Collins went on. 'I must assume you wish to increase my love by suspense, in the usual manner of elegant females. I shall lead you to the church before long!'

Elizabeth did not know what else to say. There was only one thing left she could think to do – she got up and walked quickly out of the room.

No sooner had she gone than Mrs Bennet, who had been lurking nearby, rushed into the room to congratulate Mr Collins. But when Mr Collins told her what Elizabeth had said, she looked startled. She did not believe for one minute that Elizabeth's refusal was as the result of what Mr

Collins called her 'bashful modesty and delicacy of character'.

'I will speak to her and make her see reason,' she said at once. 'She is a very headstrong and foolish girl.'

But by now, Mr Collins was beginning to feel a little unsure himself. 'If she really is headstrong and foolish, perhaps she would not make a very good wife for me after all,' he muttered.

'Oh, you misunderstand me,' said Mrs Bennet in a great hurry. 'Lizzy is only headstrong about things like this. In everything else she is as good-natured as can be. Let me talk to Mr Bennet, and we will soon settle everything.'

She did not give him time to reply, but instead rushed straight to the library. 'Mr Bennet! You must come and make Lizzy marry Mr Collins,' she announced breathlessly.

Mr Bennet looked up from his book. 'Whatever are you talking about?' he asked calmly.

'Mr Collins and Lizzy!' Mrs Bennet burst out impatiently. '*She* says she will not marry him – and if you do not hurry, *he* will change his mind and decide he will not marry *her*.'

'Then what am I to do about it? It sounds like a hopeless case,' said Mr Bennet with a shrug.

'You must speak to Lizzy about it. Tell her that you *insist* upon her marrying him.'

'Very well. Call her and I'll tell her what I think,' Mr Bennet agreed.

Elizabeth was summoned into the library. 'Come here, my child,' said her father gently, as she appeared. 'I understand Mr Collins has offered to marry you. Is it true?'

'It is,' said Elizabeth shortly.

'And you have refused him?'

'I have.'

'Very well. We now come to the point. Your mother insists upon you accepting him – is that true, Mrs Bennet?'

'Yes – or I will *never see her again*!' said Mrs Bennet dramatically.

'Hmmm. Well, a difficult choice is before you, Elizabeth. From this day, you will be a stranger to one of your parents. Your mother will never see you again if you do *not* marry Mr Collins. And I will never see you again if you *do*!'

# CHAPTER NINE

Mrs Bennet flew at once into a furious temper with her husband. 'You promised me to *insist* upon her marrying him,' she cried.

But Mr Bennet had already turned back to his book. Elizabeth couldn't help grinning. She knew that her father understood exactly why she couldn't possibly marry Mr Collins.

Mrs Bennet, however, was not going to give up so easily. She was determined that Elizabeth should accept Mr Collins's proposal, and she did everything she could think of to try and convince her. First she coaxed, then she threatened, then she shouted, and then she wept. But all the while, Elizabeth remained firm.

At last, Mrs Bennet returned to Mr Collins, downcast, saying in a doleful voice, 'Oh, Mr Collins . . .'

But while she had been gone, Mr Collins had been mulling over everything Elizabeth had said to him. He still did not understand how she could possibly have refused his proposal, but he was beginning to feel indignant – and insulted.

'My dear madam,' he said brusquely, turning away from Mrs Bennet. 'Let us speak no more on the subject.'

While all this was going on, Charlotte Lucas arrived to pay the Bennets a visit. She was met by Lydia in the hallway.

'You'll never guess what has happened,' Lydia whispered excitedly. 'Mr Collins has offered to marry Lizzy – but she has said no!'

Charlotte was astonished. She followed Lydia into the breakfast room, where Mrs Bennet was now sitting by herself at the table, looking very miserable and melancholy indeed. 'Oh, Miss Lucas,' she cried. 'I hope *you* will be on my side. No one else feels anything for my poor nerves!'

Just then, Elizabeth came into the room, and Mrs Bennet glared at her. 'Here she comes, thinking nothing of any of us. All she cares about is getting her own way. Well, I tell you something, Miss Lizzy – if you continue to behave like this, you will never get a husband at all! And then I do not know *who* will look after you when your father is dead!'

It was an awkward visit for Charlotte. Elizabeth was uncomfortable and embarrassed; Mrs Bennet was peevish and cross; and as for Mr Collins, he was now simmering with resentment, refusing to either look at or speak to Elizabeth. Instead, he turned all his attentions to Charlotte herself, who politely listened to all his long and boring speeches.

'Thank you, Charlotte,' said Elizabeth gratefully before her friend left. 'It's very kind of you to help keep him in a good temper.'

Charlotte said that of course she was happy to do anything she could. But the truth was that there was more to her efforts than simply helping her friend. As soon as she'd heard that Elizabeth had refused Mr Collins's proposal of marriage, she'd begun to have an idea of her own . . .

Elizabeth hadn't the least idea what her friend was thinking until the next day, when Mr Collins slipped out early for a visit to Lucas Lodge. There, he received a very flattering welcome from Charlotte, and he had soon thrown himself at her feet.

Just as soon as Mr Collins's long speeches would allow, everything was settled. Mr Collins would marry Charlotte Lucas, and Sir William and Lady Lucas gave their delighted agreement. Lady Lucas was thrilled to have a husband for her daughter, and at once began to calculate how much longer Mr Bennet was likely to live, imagining her daughter the mistress of Longbourn.

As for Charlotte herself, she was calm and composed. She knew that Mr Collins would not be a very sensible husband and that his company would often be irritating. But she also knew she would have a comfortable life with him and looked forward with pleasure to becoming the mistress of her own home. The only thing that she regretted was that her friend Elizabeth was certain to be shocked by this sudden turn of events – and in this she was absolutely right.

'Engaged! To Mr Collins! My dear Charlotte – impossible!' Elizabeth cried out, when Charlotte told her the news.

'But why should you think so?' asked Charlotte in a matter-of-fact voice. 'Just because you don't want to marry Mr Collins doesn't mean that no one else would.'

Comfortable home Security Happiness

Conceited Pompous Definitely not husband material

Realising she was serious, Elizabeth pulled herself together and tried to wish her friend every happiness. But Charlotte was not fooled. 'I know you are surprised – especially as Mr Collins so recently wished to marry you,' she said. 'But when you've had time to think it over, I hope you'll understand. I'm not romantic, you know – I never was. All I want is a comfortable home, and I know Mr Collins can give me that. I think my chance of happiness with him is as good as it would be with anyone else.'

But although she nodded politely, Elizabeth could still scarcely believe what Charlotte was doing. 'She knows what Mr Collins is like,' she protested to Jane. 'How can she bear to be his wife? It is so humiliating.'

'Well, Charlotte is very different from you or I,' said Jane more understandingly. 'Perhaps she does really care for him.'

But Elizabeth just snorted. 'I can't believe that. Mr Collins is a conceited, pompous, silly sort of man as well you know. I can't think of any good reason for marrying him.'

As for Mrs Bennet, she was perfectly horrified. 'But Mr Collins wants to marry *Lizzy*!' she exclaimed. At first, she refused to believe it; then she insisted that Mr Collins had been tricked by Charlotte; next, she declared that they would never be happy together; and finally that the engagement was certain to be broken off. Most of all, she was convinced that the whole thing was Elizabeth's fault, and a full week went by before she could see Elizabeth without scolding her. Meanwhile, Kitty and Lydia giggled together at the thought of how awful it would be to marry Mr Collins, and enjoyed themselves spreading the news of Charlotte's engagement around Meryton.

As for Lady Lucas, even after Mr Collins had returned home to prepare for the wedding, she called at Longbourn rather more often than usual. She spoke of how happy she was, and how wonderful it would be to have a daughter married – apparently not noticing Mrs Bennet's sour looks and rude remarks.

The engagement of Mr Collins and Charlotte Lucas was not the only piece of unexpected news to come to Longbourn that week. One morning at breakfast, a letter was delivered from Netherfield for Jane. It contained a little sheet of elegant notepaper, and Elizabeth noticed Jane's face change as she read it. However, her sister quickly put the letter into her pocket, and joined in the conversation in her usual way. It was not until she and Elizabeth were by themselves that she took out the letter again.

'This is from Miss Bingley – and it has taken me very much by surprise,' she said, her usually cheerful face now anxious and unhappy. 'They have all left Netherfield and are now on their way to town – with no plans to come back again!'

'I'm sure Mr Bingley won't stay in London for long,' said Elizabeth reassuringly.

But Jane shook her head. 'Miss Bingley says quite clearly that none of them will return this winter. And that's not all,' she went on, miserably. 'Listen to *this*:

*Mr Darcy is impatient to see his sister, Georgiana, as are Mrs Hurst and I. Miss Darcy has no equal for beauty* *and elegance, and we both hope very much that she may soon become <u>our</u> sister. My brother admires her greatly, and he will have much opportunity of seeing her when we are all in town. Am I wrong, my dearest Jane, to hope for an event that will bring happiness to so many?'*

Jane looked up at Elizabeth in despair. 'It is perfectly clear! Miss Bingley is convinced her brother doesn't care about me, but she guesses my feelings for him, and she means, most kindly, to warn me that he prefers Miss Darcy.'

Elizabeth took the letter from her sister's hand and frowned over it. 'That's not what I think at all,' she declared bluntly. 'If you ask me, Miss Bingley knows her brother is in love with you but she wants him to marry Miss Darcy. She hopes he will stay in town and has written this to try and persuade you that he doesn't care about you.'

Jane shook her head and sighed sadly.

'You have to believe me, Jane,' Elizabeth insisted. 'No one who has seen you and Mr Bingley together could doubt how much he likes you. We are not rich or grand enough for Miss Bingley, that's all. But it won't be so easy for her to change her brother's mind. He may well admire Mr Darcy's sister – but Miss Bingley can hardly persuade him to fall in love with *her*, when he is already in love with *you*.'

'I don't believe Miss Bingley could ever behave like that.' Jane sighed again. 'The only thing I can hope is that she has been misled about her brother's feelings.'

Elizabeth wished that just for once, Jane wasn't so inclined to think that everyone was as kind and well-meaning as she was herself.

Elizabeth felt certain that Mr Bingley would soon return to Netherfield, whatever Miss Bingley might say about it. But day after day passed, and then at last, Jane received another letter. This time Miss Bingley wrote that they were all to remain in London over the winter. The letter also contained even more praise for Mr Darcy's sister, Miss Georgiana.

'That settles it. I will do my best to forget about Mr Bingley,' said Jane firmly. 'I must have made a mistake in thinking he had any feelings for me. Well, it is in the past now – and luckily there has been no harm to anyone but myself.'

Elizabeth could see that Jane was unhappy. She felt impressed by her sister's strength but very angry indeed with Mr Bingley.

'You mustn't blame him for what happened between us,' protested Jane. 'I'm quite sure he didn't mean to cause me any unhappiness.'

'But he did anyway, through his thoughtlessness,' said Elizabeth crossly. 'And I certainly blame his sisters for the part they have played in all this!'

After that, Elizabeth tried not to talk about Mr Bingley to spare her sister's feelings. Unfortunately, rarely an hour went by when Mrs Bennet didn't mention his name or wonder impatiently when he would come back to Netherfield again.

Whenever she was not talking of Mr Bingley, Mrs Bennet was bemoaning the marriage of Mr Collins and Charlotte. 'To think that Charlotte Lucas should one day be the mistress of this house,' she lamented to Mr Bennet. 'To think that I should be forced to make way for *her* and live to see her take my place.'

'My dear, do not give in to such gloomy thoughts. Let us hope for better things,' said Mr Bennet, with a mischievous grin. 'After all, perhaps I may outlive you?'

At the very thought of this, Mrs Bennet began to wail into her handkerchief.

# CHAPTER TEN

After all the upheaval of the past few weeks, it was a relief to Elizabeth when Mrs Bennet's brother and his wife, Mr and Mrs Gardiner, arrived to spend Christmas with the Bennets. Elizabeth was very fond of her aunt and uncle: Mr Gardiner was sensible and kindly, and Mrs Gardiner a great favourite with all the family.

Mrs Bennet could not wait to tell them all about her grievances and complaints. 'I have been so ill-used since I saw you last,' she sighed. 'Just think – *two* of the girls were almost married, but nothing came of it. I don't blame Jane at all for what happened with Mr Bingley. But *Lizzy*! It is very hard to think she might have been Mr Collins's wife by now. He proposed to her in this very room – and she refused him. Now Lady Lucas will have a daughter married before I do – who will one day be the mistress of this house. But the Lucases are such sly people. They are out for what they can get.' She heaved an enormous sigh and dabbed at her brow with her handkerchief. 'It makes me very ill to be so thwarted by my own family and neighbours. My poor nerves! But you coming just now is a great comfort – and I am very glad to hear what you have to tell us about the new fashion for long sleeves,' she added to Mrs Gardiner.

Mrs Gardiner listened to Mrs Bennet patiently. When she was alone with Elizabeth, she said, 'Poor Jane. What happened with Mr Bingley must have been very upsetting for her. I wonder, do you think she would like to come back to London with us for a visit? A change of scene might help. She wouldn't have to worry about bumping into Mr Bingley unexpectedly – after all we live in a very different part of town, and have quite different friends.'

Elizabeth thought this was an excellent idea. A change was just what Jane needed, and Mrs Gardiner was right: there was not much chance of Mr Darcy or even Miss Bingley turning up at the Gardiners' quite ordinary house on Gracechurch Street. It was a world away from the grand parts of London they were no doubt used to!

Soon it was agreed that Jane would return to London with Mr and Mrs Gardiner in the New Year. The rest of their stay was packed with Christmas festivities: carol-singing, supper parties and all kinds of cosy celebrations. For these, they were joined by friends and neighbours including the Lucases, Mrs Phillips, and of course all the officers – in particular Mr Wickham, who was by now a great favourite with all the Bennets, and especially with Elizabeth.

'It's such a shame Mr Wickham has no money of his own and can't afford to marry as yet,' said Mrs Gardiner quietly to Mrs Bennet. 'Such an interesting and charming young man could have made just the right husband for Lizzy.'

'Hmph,' said Mrs Bennet, who was still cross with Elizabeth after all that had happened with Mr Collins.

Not long after the Gardiners had said goodbye and gone back to London, taking Jane with them, Charlotte came to Longbourn to say farewell before she left to be married.

Mrs Bennet managed to say grudgingly in a bad-tempered tone that she 'wished she would be happy' but Charlotte didn't seem to notice her rudeness. Her attention was fixed on Elizabeth. 'I hope you will write to me often,' she said, looking rather anxious. 'And will you come and see me in my new home? My sister Maria is to come and pay me a visit in the spring, and I would like it very much if you could join her.'

Elizabeth said that she would – though she did not in the least relish the thought of going to visit Mr Collins.

She soon had a letter from Jane to say that she had arrived safely in London. Jane also wrote that she had sent a note to Miss Bingley to let her know she was in town and to invite her to visit, but that she had received no reply.

It was not for several weeks that Jane wrote to Elizabeth about Miss Bingley again.

*I must admit, Lizzy, that you were right all along. I have been completely misled by Miss Bingley. She did not visit until yesterday, nor send any note, although I have waited at home for her every morning for a fortnight. When at last she came, it was obvious she took no pleasure in seeing me. She made a slight apology for not calling before, and didn't say a word about wishing to see me again. She could not have been more different, after behaving before as though we were the best of friends!*

*She made it quite clear that Mr Bingley knows I am in town, but that he is very busy at present with Mr Darcy and his sister. I can't help thinking that if he at all cared for me, he would have come to see me weeks ago . . .*

The letter made Elizabeth feel even more sorry for her sister, although she was glad that Jane would no longer be taken in by Miss Bingley. Most of all, she felt bitterly disappointed in Mr Bingley. She

began to hope he *would* marry Miss Darcy, who
Mr Wickham had described as being very much
like her brother, proud and unpleasant – and would
no doubt make his life very miserable indeed.

# CHAPTER ELEVEN

January and February soon passed by. Elizabeth wrote to Jane to tell her all that was happening at Longbourn – and in particular to share news of Mr Wickham. He no longer spent so much time with Elizabeth, for he had begun paying attentions to a young lady named Mary King, who had recently inherited a great deal of money. But Elizabeth was able to write to Jane about it without much pain or sadness. It was true that she had liked Mr Wickham very much, but she hadn't fallen in love with him. What was more, she could understand that a charming but poor young man might well be tempted by the idea of marrying a pleasant young lady who had ten thousand pounds to her name.

In any case, she was soon to depart on her trip to see Charlotte and Mr Collins. She had not much wanted to go at first, but she soon found that Charlotte was determined.

When she arrived at the Parsonage with Charlotte's younger sister Maria, Mr Collins and Charlotte were waiting for them at the door. Charlotte was obviously delighted to see them, whilst Mr Collins was exactly the same as ever, making them a long and formal speech of welcome, and telling them all about his 'humble abode'. He pointed out every article of furniture, from the sideboard to the coal-bucket, and even opened a closet to proudly display some shelves which he had fitted on Lady Catherine's own advice.

Elizabeth guessed that these remarks were mostly addressed to her – perhaps to remind her of all she had lost in turning down his proposal of marriage. But no sideboard nor coal-bucket nor shelves in the closet could possibly make her regret not marrying Mr Collins!

Of course, it did not take long for Mr Collins to bring the conversation back to his favourite subject. 'You will have the honour of seeing Lady Catherine on Sunday at church and I know you will be delighted with her,' he began. 'I am sure she will include you in every invitation that she honours us with during your stay. We dine at Rosings twice a week, and are never allowed to walk home. Her Ladyship's carriage is always ordered for us − I should say, *one* of Her Ladyship's carriages, for of course, she has several,' he added grandly.

'Lady Catherine is a very attentive neighbour,' agreed Charlotte politely.

'Very true, my dear, that is exactly what I say,' declared Mr Collins, nodding vigorously.

The next day, while Elizabeth was in her bedroom, there was a sudden noise downstairs

which seemed to send the whole house into confusion. After a moment, she heard somebody running upstairs calling her name. She came out on to the landing to find Maria, breathless and agitated. 'Make haste and come to the window, for there is such a sight to be seen!' she exclaimed.

When Elizabeth hurried after her to the window, she saw that Charlotte and Mr Collins were standing at the garden gate to speak with two ladies who were sitting in a grand carriage. 'Is this all?' she said, with a laugh. 'I expected that at least the pigs had got into the garden, but it is only Lady Catherine and her daughter.'

'Oh no, *that* is not Lady Catherine!' said Maria, quite shocked by the suggestion. 'The older lady is Mrs Jenkinson, who lives with them. The other is Miss de Bourgh.'

'She is very rude, to keep Charlotte standing outside in all this wind,' objected Elizabeth. 'Why doesn't she come inside?'

'Oh, she hardly ever does. Charlotte says it is the very greatest of favours when Miss de Bourgh comes in.'

Elizabeth looked at Miss de Bourgh's bad-tempered expression, remembering that Mr Wickham had told her she was supposed to marry Mr Darcy. 'Yes, she will do very well . . . she will make him a perfect wife,' she said to herself.

Before Maria could ask her who she was talking

about, Mr Collins came back into the house, delighted to share the news that they had all been invited to dine at Rosings the very next day.

Mr Collins could hardly talk about anything else for the whole of that day, or the next morning. He spent most of the time telling them what they could expect to see at Rosings. This, he explained, was so they would not be overwhelmed by the fine rooms, the servants or the splendid dinner.

'And don't feel uneasy about your appearance, my dear cousin,' he told Elizabeth fussily, as she went to get dressed for dinner. 'Lady Catherine would never expect *you* to be as elegant as she is. She won't think any of the worse of you for being simply dressed.'

While they were all getting ready, he came several times to their bedroom doors to remind them to be quick, as Lady Catherine disliked being kept waiting. As they walked up to the great house, he was still talking: of Lady Catherine, of the beauties of the park, of the house itself – even detailing the cost of the windows. It was no wonder that by the time they arrived Maria looked quite terrified. But Elizabeth's courage did not fail her.

She looked curiously at Lady Catherine, as they came into the room where she was sitting with her daughter and Mrs Jenkinson. Lady Catherine was a tall woman with a haughty manner. She talked a great deal, and every word she said was spoken with great determination, as though there was no possible way she could ever be wrong about anything. Elizabeth at once recognised a resemblance to her nephew, Mr Darcy. Beside her, Miss de Bourgh seemed rather small, and spoke hardly at all.

The dinner was delicious, and Mr Collins took every opportunity of admiring it, praising every dish. Maria, over-awed by Lady Catherine, did not dare to say a single word. There was little to do but listen to Lady Catherine talk, giving her opinion on every subject, including how Charlotte should best look after her home, her garden, and even her cows and chickens.

After a while, Lady Catherine turned her attention to Elizabeth, asking a great many questions about how many sisters she had, whether any of them were likely to be married soon, where they had been educated, and even what carriage her father kept. Elizabeth tried to answer her politely.

'Do you play the piano and sing, Miss Bennet?' asked Lady Catherine.

'A little.'

'And do your sisters play and sing?'

'One of them does.'

'Why did you not all learn? You ought all to have learned. Do you draw?'

'No, not at all.'

'What, none of you? That is most strange! Your

mother should have taken you to town to learn from the drawing-masters there. Did your governess not teach you?'

'We never had a governess.'

'No governess! How is that possible? I never heard of such a thing,' tutted Lady Catherine. 'Are any of your younger sisters out in society?'

'Yes ma'am, all of them.'

'All! What, all five at once? The younger ones out before the older ones are married? That is very odd. Your youngest sisters must be *very* young.'

'My youngest sister is only fifteen,' Elizabeth agreed. 'But I think it would be hard on younger sisters to stop them enjoying society and amusement, just because their elder sisters haven't married early.'

Lady Catherine looked indignant. 'Upon my word!' she exclaimed. 'You give your opinion very decidedly for a young person.'

To Elizabeth's relief, it was then time to retire

to the drawing room to play a game of cards. But she noticed that for the rest of the evening, Lady Catherine occasionally gave her a sharp, beady-eyed look as if she was trying to work out what to make of her.

# CHAPTER TWELVE

This was not to be Elizabeth's only visit to Rosings Park. In fact, during the month that she stayed with Charlotte and Mr Collins, they were all invited to dine with Lady Catherine several times a week.

It was at one of these dinners that Elizabeth learned that Mr Darcy was soon to pay a visit to his aunt. Although she could not say she was looking forward to seeing him again, she did think it might be rather amusing to observe him at Rosings. It was obvious that Lady Catherine was immensely proud of her nephew and she talked of his visit with great satisfaction.

A few days later, Mr Darcy arrived, together with another of Lady Catherine's nephews, Colonel Fitzwilliam. Elizabeth thought Colonel Fitzwilliam was not at all like his cousin: in fact, he was as friendly and warm as Mr Darcy was cold and distant. At their next dinner at Rosings, Mr Darcy hardly spoke to her – but the Colonel came at once to sit beside Elizbeth, and began talking to her about travelling, books and music. In fact, they got on so well together that after a short time, Lady Catherine began to look cross.

'What are you saying, Fitzwilliam? What are you telling Miss Bennet? Let me hear what it is. I must have my share of the conversation,' she insisted.

'We are talking about music,' said Colonel Fitzwilliam.

'Oh, music! There are few people in England who have more true enjoyment of music than I do.' Lady Catherine sniffed. 'Or more talent . . .

that is, of course, if I had ever had the opportunity to learn to play . . .'

'Well, Miss Bennet is going to play for us now,' said Colonel Fitzwilliam smilingly. But when Elizabeth went over to the piano, Lady Catherine only listened to half the song, and then went on talking. Mr Darcy, on the other hand, paced over to the piano and then stood beside her in silence, a frown on his face.

'Are you trying to frighten me, Mr Darcy, by coming over to watch me play?' Elizabeth asked with a smile.

'Of course not,' said Mr Darcy gruffly.

'Miss Bennet would not play at all badly if she would practise more, and had the advantage of a London teacher,' Lady Catherine could be heard saying in a loud voice across the room.

It was all decidedly uncomfortable, and Elizabeth felt relieved when it was time to go home.

But that was not the last she saw of Mr Darcy and Colonel Fitzwilliam. In fact, they began calling at the Parsonage every day. It was obvious that Colonel Fitzwilliam was eager for some cheerful company – but it was more difficult to understand why Mr Darcy came so often. He didn't seem to enjoy the visits very much, standing stiffly and saying little, even when Colonel Fitzwilliam joked and teased him.

Elizabeth was glad of the Colonel's lively

company. There was only so much of Lady Catherine and Mr Collins that she could put up with! On her daily rambles through the grounds of Rosings Park, she would sometimes meet him, and they would continue walking together, talking pleasantly of this or that. The conversation always seemed to flow quite easily – until one morning, Colonel Fitzwilliam happened to mention Mr Bingley.

'He seems a very pleasant, gentleman-like man. I know he is a great friend of Darcy's,' he remarked.

'Oh yes,' said Elizabeth with a quick grin. 'They are not at all alike, but Mr Darcy is very kind to Mr Bingley, and takes very good care of him.'

The Colonel grinned back. 'You're quite right there. Mr Darcy *does* take good care of him. In fact, I believe he congratulates himself on having recently saved him from a very unsuitable marriage.'

Elizabeth almost gasped aloud. Surely this could only refer to Jane? 'Did Mr Darcy say why he interfered?' she asked quickly.

'Oh, I understand there were strong objections to the lady,' said the Colonel, looking vague.

Elizabeth fell silent. She had always assumed Miss Bingley was the one who had kept Jane and Mr Bingley apart – now she knew that it was Mr Darcy who was the cause of all Jane's unhappiness!

She decided not to join the others on their visit to Rosings that afternoon, saying she had a headache. After what she had learned, she could not bear to spend any more time politely drinking tea and trying to make conversation with Mr Darcy.

But after the others had all gone out, and she sat by herself at the Parsonage, she was disturbed by a sudden sharp knock at the door.

To her enormous surprise, Mr Darcy himself came hurrying into the room. He came over to her at once.

'I have struggled, but my feelings will not be repressed. You must allow me to tell you how ardently I admire and love you.'

# CHAPTER THIRTEEN

Elizabeth could hardly believe her ears. She was so astonished that for several minutes, she said nothing, only gaped at Mr Darcy while he spoke of how his love for her had swept away all his objections to her family and to her lowly position in society.

'In spite of all my efforts, I cannot conquer my feelings for you,' he declared, staring at her intently. 'And so – I have come here to offer you my hand in marriage.'

Elizabeth stared back at him. She could see from his face that he had no doubt that she would say 'yes' – for he was rich and important, and she was neither. Well, he was in for a shock. Her face felt very hot as she replied, 'I'm sorry to give pain to anyone, but I must refuse. I'm quite sure, given all that you've said, that any feelings you may have for me won't last very long.'

Mr Darcy turned pale with surprise, and then with anger at this terse response. 'That is your answer?' he spluttered. 'You aren't even going to tell me *why* you are rejecting me?'

Elizabeth glared at him. 'Do you really think it is likely I would agree to marry the person who has ruined my sister's happiness?'

It was clear Mr Darcy knew exactly what she meant. He did not look in the least bit sorry as she demanded, 'Do you deny it?'

'I don't wish to deny it,' he replied. 'I did everything I could to separate Mr Bingley from your sister. I have been kinder to him than I have to myself.'

Elizabeth felt angrier than ever. 'And that's not all! Then there's the way you behaved to Mr Wickham!'

'Oh, you take an interest in that gentleman's concerns, do you?'

'Anyone who hears of his misfortunes would take an interest.'

'His misfortunes,' repeated Mr Darcy in a voice full of sarcasm. 'Yes, his *misfortunes* have been great indeed.'

'You denied him the life he should have had, and yet, you speak of his misfortunes so casually – with contempt and ridicule.'

Mr Darcy turned away from her. 'So this is your opinion of me? I thank you for explaining.' He turned back to stare at Elizabeth. 'But I think you would have overlooked all this if I had flattered you. Had I not been honest about my efforts to overcome my feelings for you. But I pride myself on always being truthful. Besides, you could hardly expect me to rejoice in your relations or their position in society, so far below my own.'

Elizabeth could feel herself growing more and more furious with every moment that passed, but she battled to stay calm as she replied, 'You are wrong – the insulting way you proposed only spared me the concern I might have felt in refusing, had you behaved in a more gentleman-like manner.

You could not have made me an offer of marriage in any way that would have tempted me to accept it.' Mr Darcy's expression was astonished – and rather hurt – but she ploughed on. 'You are conceited and selfish. I had not known you for a month before I felt sure you were the last man on earth who I could *ever* marry.'

But here Mr Darcy interrupted her. 'You have said quite enough. I understand your feelings. I am sorry to have taken up your time,' he said and hastily left the room.

Elizabeth told no one about Mr Darcy's proposal. She still found it hard to believe it had happened at all. She had actually received an offer of marriage from Mr Darcy! He had said he had been secretly in love with her for many months. But her amazement was mixed together with furious anger at his pride and at his behaviour to Jane and to Mr Wickham.

She still felt very agitated the next morning and decided to go out for a walk to calm her thoughts. As she made her way through the grounds of Rosings Park – now becoming greener and more pleasant as spring approached – she caught sight of a gentleman standing beneath the trees ahead of her. Not wanting to speak to anyone, even Colonel Fitzwilliam, she turned quickly away – but the person had already seen her, and stepped forward, calling out her name. It was Mr Darcy, holding a letter in his outstretched hand.

'I have been walking here in the hope of meeting you. Will you do me the honour of reading this letter?' he said briefly. Then with a slight bow he turned and walked away, and was soon out of sight.

Elizabeth looked in surprise at the envelope she was holding. As she walked back along the lane, she opened it and began to read:

*Do not be afraid – this letter will not contain any repeat of the things I said to you yesterday. However, you made two accusations: firstly, that regardless of either of their feelings, I separated Mr Bingley from your sister; and secondly, that I cruelly damaged the prospects of Mr Wickham. I now wish to have the chance to explain myself.*

*I had not long been at Netherfield before I saw how much Bingley admired your sister, but it was not until the ball there that I realised he had fallen in love with her. However, although your sister received his attentions with pleasure, she showed no special feelings for him – and I guessed her heart would not be easily touched.*

*But this was not my only objection to the idea of their marriage. I knew it would be unsuitable because of the improper behaviour of the rest of your family – your mother, your three younger sisters, and even occasionally your father. Pardon me: it pains me to offend you, but it is true.*

*In London, Mr Bingley's sisters and I pointed this out to him, and persuaded him that he should not return to Netherfield. I don't blame myself for doing so, but I do now wonder if it was right to keep from him the news that your sister had come to London. Perhaps this concealment was beneath me.*

*The case of Mr Wickham is more complicated, as I do not know exactly what he has accused me of. However, I will tell you the whole history of his connection with my family:*

*Mr Wickham is the son of my father's steward. My father supported him through school and university, and afterwards wished to help him go into the church. He was very fond of Mr Wickham, but as we grew older, I began to see a very a different – far less pleasant – side of my childhood companion.*

*When my father died, he left money to Mr Wickham, and had also arranged a job for him as a parson. But within a few months of my father's death,*

*Mr Wickham wrote to me and said he had decided he did not want to go into the church after all, and asked if more money could be given to him instead of the job my father had arranged. He told me he planned to go to London to study law, and I agreed to help him, feeling sure that Mr Wickham was not at all well-suited to being a clergyman.*

*But his studying law soon turned out to be a pretence, and his life in town was idle and full of wickedness. Before long he wrote to me again, demanding more money. This time, I refused. He was resentful and angry – but for a while I heard little from him, until last summer when he suddenly reappeared.*

*My sister Georgiana is more than ten years younger than me and since my father's death, Colonel Fitzwilliam and I have been her guardians. She spent last summer at the seaside in Ramsgate, and Mr Wickham secretly followed her there. He managed to persuade her that she was in love with him, and that they should run away together to be married. She was only fifteen years old.*

*Luckily, I arrived unexpectedly a day or two before the planned wedding, and Georgiana told me the truth. I knew that Mr Wickham wanted my sister's fortune of thirty thousand pounds – but also to revenge himself on me. Thank goodness I arrived in time to prevent their running away together.*

*These events were never made publicly known, for my sister's sake – and I know I can trust you to keep this story a secret. However, you now know the truth of all my dealings with Mr Wickham. Colonel Fitzwilliam can confirm everything I have written here.*

As she read this letter, Elizabeth was first overwhelmed with anger all over again. How dare Mr Darcy presume that her sister had no real feelings for Mr Bingley? It was true enough that Jane was often calm and serene, and didn't always show her emotions. But why should it be up to

Mr Darcy to decide how she felt, and to keep her and Mr Bingley apart?

Then she saw what Mr Darcy had written about her family and her anger began to fade. Instead, she felt a horrible shock of recognition, thinking of how they had behaved at the Netherfield ball.

Her cheeks turned red with embarrassment all over again, as she remembered her mother's loud remarks about 'rich men', and Lydia and Kitty romping and flirting with the officers. It was awful to think that Jane's disappointment had been caused by her own family.

But by the time she reached the section of the letter about Mr Wickham, she had forgotten her anger and embarrassment altogether. She could hardly believe what she was reading. Surely it couldn't be true that the amiable Mr Wickham had really devised such a scheme? But Mr Darcy had said that Colonel Fitzwilliam would confirm everything he had written, and Elizabeth felt certain she could trust the Colonel. Besides, Mr Darcy would surely never make up a story like that about his own sister.

All at once, Elizabeth remembered her first conversation with Mr Wickham when he had told her his history. Now she thought about it again, it seemed odd that he had confided so much in a stranger. Then she recalled how he had avoided the ball at Netherfield when he had known Mr Darcy would be there, how Miss Bingley had warned her against him, and how he had paid attentions to the wealthy Miss King. Though he might seem so charming, she began to realise that she knew very little about Mr Wickham, his friends, or his life before he had arrived in Meryton. On the other hand, it was clear that many people who had known him for a long time respected and trusted Mr Darcy – like Mr Bingley, Colonel Fitzwilliam and even Lady Catherine herself.

Had she really been so prejudiced by her dislike of Mr Darcy that she had allowed Mr Wickham to trick and mislead her? The more she thought about it, the more ashamed Elizabeth felt. She had always prided herself on being a sharp observer of those around her – now, she felt like a fool.

She walked and walked for a long time, reading the letter over and over again. It was only when she realised how long she had been gone that she hurried back to the Parsonage. There, she found that the two gentlemen from Rosings had each called in her absence. Mr Darcy had waited for her for only a few minutes, Charlotte told her, but

Colonel Fitzwilliam had stayed for over an hour, hoping for her return.

Elizabeth was not sorry she had missed him. She couldn't think about pleasant conversations with the Colonel now: she could only think of Mr Darcy's letter.

# CHAPTER FOURTEEN

Mr Darcy and Colonel Fitzwilliam left Rosings the next morning. After everything that had happened, Elizabeth felt relieved to see them go, but Lady Catherine was not at all happy.

'I feel it exceedingly,' she announced that evening at dinner. 'I am so attached to these young men – and they are very attached to me. They were excessively sorry to go. The dear Colonel rallied his spirits, but Darcy seemed to feel it most acutely. His attachment to Rosings grows stronger each year!'

She looked fondly at her daughter, as if she believed it was Miss de Bourgh that made Mr Darcy so attached to Rosings. Elizabeth looked down at her plate, wondering what Lady Catherine would think if she knew the truth about what had caused Mr Darcy's mood. And just imagine what she would have said if Elizabeth had been presented to her as her nephew's future bride!

Lady Catherine noticed her thoughtful face. 'You are rather out of spirits, Miss Bennet,' she observed sharply. 'But then I suppose you must be sorry to soon be going home yourself. You must write to your mother to ask if you can stay a little longer. I am sure she can spare you another fortnight.'

'Perhaps, but my father cannot. He wrote last week to hurry my return,' said Elizabeth quickly.

Lady Catherine thought nothing of that. 'Your father can spare you if your mother can – daughters are never much consequence to fathers. And if you will stay another month, I will take you as far as London myself in the barouche!'

Mr Collins was all of a twitter at the generosity of this offer – but it did not tempt Elizabeth in the least. She had had quite enough of Rosings and Lady Catherine. She spent most of her last few days walking in the park, thinking over Mr Darcy's letter – which she now knew more or less by heart.

At last, the day came for their departure: the trunks were packed, and the chaise was at the gate.

'It gives me great pleasure to think you have passed your time here agreeably,' said Mr Collins to Elizabeth, as they said farewell in the garden. 'You have seen what a wonderful situation we have here – and what a footing we are on with Lady Catherine and her family. You have seen what kind attentions Lady Catherine pays to Mrs Collins!' He lowered his voice. 'Altogether, I hope—' And here he broke off. 'Well, perhaps on *that* point it is as well to be silent. But let me assure you, Miss Elizabeth, that I can from my heart wish you the same happiness in marriage that I have experienced. My dear Charlotte and I share one mind, and one way of thinking. We seem to have been designed for each other,' he simpered, as across the room, Charlotte smiled a little uncomfortably.

Elizabeth thought it was rather dreadful to leave her with only Mr Collins for company. But Charlotte had chosen him as her husband, and although she was sorry to see her visitors go, she seemed very happy in her new home. As they drove away, she waved goodbye, whilst Mr Collins called out anxiously that he would be sure to deliver their humble respects and grateful thanks to Lady Catherine.

'Good gracious!' exclaimed Maria, as the carriage rumbled off. 'It seems only a day or two since we first arrived – and just think how many things have happened. Oh, how much I shall have to tell!'

To herself, Elizabeth added: *And how much I shall have to conceal!*

Several hours later, they drew up to the inn where Mr Bennet's carriage was to meet them to take them on the final stage of the journey home.

Elizabeth saw at once that two familiar faces were waving to them from the dining-room window. It was Lydia and Kitty, who had come to meet them – and proudly displayed a table set out with cold meat and salads.

'Isn't this a nice surprise?' said Lydia. 'We're going to treat you. But you must give us the money because we have spent all ours. Look, I bought this bonnet – I don't think it's very pretty but I thought I might as well buy it. I shall pull it to pieces as soon as I get home and see if I can make it up any better.'

'It's very ugly, isn't it, Lizzy?' said Kitty with a giggle.

'Oh, but there were two or three much uglier in the shop. Anyway, it will not matter what anyone wears this summer, since the soldiers are leaving Meryton!' went on Lydia woefully. 'They are going to Brighton. I do so want Papa to take us there for the summer. It would be such a delicious scheme and I daresay it would hardly cost anything at all.'

But before Elizabeth could say anything about this, Kitty cut in. 'Oh Lizzy! Speaking of the officers . . . we have got some excellent news for you about a certain person we all like,' she declared.

'Mr Wickham is not to marry Mary King after all,' announced Lydia, who always wanted to be the first with any piece of news. 'She has gone to live with her uncle in Liverpool – and Wickham is safe!'

Or rather, *Mary King* was safe, thought Elizabeth, thinking of Mr Darcy's letter. But she could not say anything to her sisters about that, of course. Mr Darcy had asked her to keep his story to herself – and Lydia and Kitty were the last people she would trust with a secret.

'She is a great fool for going away, if she liked him,' observed Lydia, tucking into a large plateful of food.

'Was there a very great attachment between

them?' asked Maria, who had been listening wide-eyed to all this talk.

'Not on his side, I am sure. I don't suppose he cared three straws for her.'

Elizabeth reflected that Lydia was probably right: with all she now knew about Mr Wickham, she felt sure that all he had really been interested in was Miss King's ten thousand pounds.

As soon as they had finished eating, the whole party with their boxes, bags and parcels were squashed into the carriage and on the road towards home.

'How nicely we are crammed in,' cried Lydia. 'Now, let us hear all about what has happened to you since you went away. Have you had any flirting? I was in great hopes that you would have found a husband before you came back.'

But Elizabeth said nothing about her unexpected suitor. In fact, she didn't say very much at all. There was no chance to get a word in, for Lydia

– with hints and additions from Kitty – talked busily about all their own doings, parties and jokes all the way back to Longbourn.

When they arrived at home, Elizabeth was delighted to see that Jane had also returned from her visit to

London. The Lucas family were there too, to welcome Maria home, and the dining room was full of noise: Lady Lucas quizzing Maria about Charlotte's house; Mrs Bennet asking Jane about London fashions; and Lydia, in a voice louder than anyone else's, talking of their outing. 'Mary, you ought to have come with us. I thought I should die with laughter! We were so merry in the carriage on the way home, we talked and laughed so loud that anyone might have heard us ten miles off.'

'Such things have no charms for me,' said Mary disapprovingly. 'I should infinitely prefer a book.'

Elizabeth waited impatiently until there was a chance to get away from everyone and talk to Jane in private. At long last they were alone, and although she left out everything relating to Mr Bingley, she poured out every other detail about what had happened between herself and Mr Darcy.

She did not hesitate to tell Jane about Mr Wickham and Mr Darcy's sister. Unlike Kitty and

Lydia, she knew that Jane could be absolutely relied on to keep the secret.

'Mr Darcy proposed!' her sister exclaimed, wide-eyed with amazement as Elizabeth related the story. 'Though I'm not at all surprised that anyone should admire you,' she added at once.

But what did make Jane truly astonished was the story of Mr Wickham. 'I don't know when I have been more shocked. Poor Mr Darcy! I can hardly believe it – Mr Wickham always appears so full of goodness and openness.'

'Yes, it seems that Mr Darcy has all the goodness, but Mr Wickham all the appearance of it,' said Elizabeth with a laugh.

'But Lizzy, when you first read that letter, you couldn't have treated the matter as lightly as you do now,' said Jane, knowing that her sister had liked Mr Wickham very much indeed.

'I felt very uncomfortable,' Elizabeth admitted. 'And I had no Jane to comfort me.'

The sisters hugged for a moment, and then Elizabeth went on. 'Now, I'd like your advice on something. Should I make the truth about Mr Wickham known to everyone?'

Jane thought for a moment. 'Surely there would be no cause for that?'

Elizabeth nodded. 'And Mr Darcy hasn't given me permission to make any of this public – in fact he wanted me to keep the story about his sister a secret. Besides, Mr Wickham will soon be going away to Brighton with the regiment, so it doesn't matter very much.'

'Perhaps he is sorry for what he has done now, in any case,' said Jane hopefully.

Elizabeth felt much better once she had told Jane the truth. But at the same time, she could see that Jane herself was still unhappy. Although she didn't say a word about it, Elizabeth guessed that she was still in love with Mr Bingley, and preferred him to any other man she had ever met.

Mrs Bennet obviously thought so too. 'But I don't suppose there is any chance of her getting him now,' she sighed to Elizabeth. 'Well, he is an extremely undeserving young man. My only comfort is that Jane will die of a broken heart and then he'll be sorry for what he has done!'

A minute later, she had changed the subject. 'The Collinses live very comfortably, do they? I suppose they often talk about having this house when your father is dead. No doubt they look on it as quite their own.'

'Mama, they would hardly talk like that in front of me,' Elizabeth pointed out.

'Hmph!' Mrs Bennet was not at all consoled by this. 'I have no doubt they talk about it constantly when they're alone!'

# CHAPTER FIFTEEN

It was the final week before the regiment were due to depart for Brighton, and all the young ladies of Meryton were drooping at the thought. Kitty and Lydia were so miserable that they could not understand how their older sisters could possibly manage to eat and sleep as usual.

'What is to become of us! What are we to do?' they wailed.

Mrs Bennet shared their woe. 'I remember I cried for two days together when the regiment left when I was a girl. I thought my heart should break.'

'I am sure mine will!' said Lydia crossly. 'If we

could only go to Brighton! But Papa is so disagreeable and says he will not take us.'

'I should so much like to see Brighton – and a little sea-bathing would be certain to help my poor nerves,' said Mrs Bennet with a sidelong glance at her husband.

'I am sure it would do *me* a great deal of good,' added Kitty hopefully.

But Mr Bennet ignored them all and went on reading.

In fact, Lydia's gloom did not last long. The very next day, she received an exciting invitation from Mrs Forster, the young wife of the Colonel of the regiment. Mrs Forster and Lydia had become great friends since the regiment had been at Meryton – and now she wanted Lydia to come to Brighton with her as her guest.

Lydia was in raptures, and Mrs Bennet delighted, but Kitty – who had not been included in the invitation — burst into disappointed tears. Paying her no attention, Lydia flew joyfully about the house, already picturing the glories of Brighton, all the officers dazzling in scarlet, and herself the centre of attention, flirting with at least six of them at once.

Meanwhile, Kitty sat peevishly in the parlour. 'I can't see why Mrs Forster shouldn't ask me as well as Lydia,' she complained. 'Though I am not her *particular* friend I have just as much right to be asked — and more, for I am two years older!'

While Jane tried to console her, Elizabeth went to speak to her father in the library. Although she knew Lydia would be furious, she felt certain she should not be allowed to go Brighton. Lydia was wild enough at home — goodness knows what she would be like be in a strange town full of soldiers, with only Mrs Forster to look after her.

But Mr Bennet did not agree. 'Consider,' he said. 'Lydia will never be easy until she has made a fool of herself in some public place or other. Here is an opportunity for her to do it with little expense or inconvenience to her family.'

'If you knew the great disadvantage to us all which has already arisen from Lydia's behaviour, you would think differently,' Elizabeth protested, remembering again what Mr Darcy had written in his letter.

'Already arisen?' repeated Mr Bennet with a grin. 'What, has she frightened away some of your lovers? Poor little Lizzy! But do not be cast down. Such squeamish youths are not worth it.'

'What I mean to say is that our reputation as a family is affected by Lydia's wild behaviour,' argued Elizabeth impatiently. 'You know Kitty follows wherever Lydia leads, and if you do not do something about it now, there may be grave consequences for us all.'

Mr Bennet affectionately took her hand. 'Do not make yourself uneasy, my love,' he reassured her. 'Wherever you and Jane are known, you will be respected and valued. No one will think less of you for your sisters' behaviour. We shall have no peace at Longbourn if Lydia does not go to Brighton. Colonel Forster is a sensible man and will keep her out of any real mischief.'

And with this, Elizabeth had to be content.

★★★

On the last day before the regiment were to leave, the officers dined at Longbourn. Amongst them was Mr Wickham. He swaggered over to Elizabeth, who he had not seen for some time.

'How did you enjoy your visit to Mr Collins?' he asked, all friendliness and charm. 'Did you meet the famous Lady Catherine herself?'

'I did,' said Elizabeth. 'We spent a great deal of time at Rosings Park. Mr Darcy and his cousin Colonel Fitzwilliam were staying there – do you know the Colonel?'

Mr Wickham looked surprised and then a little uncomfortable, before smiling quickly and saying that he did. 'A very gentleman–like man. His manners are very different from his cousin's.'

'Yes, very different. But I think Mr Darcy improves on closer acquaintance,' said Elizabeth.

'Really?' cried Mr Wickham in astonishment. 'Have his manners improved and become more civil? I can't believe he is changed in essentials.'

'Oh no,' said Elizabeth with a knowing smile. 'In essentials I believe he is very much . . . as he ever was.'

Mr Wickham stared at her as she explained, 'I don't mean to imply that he has changed – rather that *me knowing him better* has helped me to understand him more.'

Mr Wickham now began to look alarmed and was silent for a few moments before flashing her with another of his smiles. 'I expect he is careful to behave well when he visits his aunt – I know he is quite afraid of her.' But shortly afterwards, he excused himself, and moved away to where Lydia and Kitty were giggling with some of the other officers.

Mr Wickham seemed as cheerful as usual for the rest of the evening, but Elizabeth noticed he made no more efforts to engage her in conversation. At the end of the evening they said farewell to one another with perfect politeness – though Elizabeth felt she would be quite happy never to see him again.

The next morning, Lydia departed for Brighton amid tears of vexation from Kitty and eager good wishes from Mrs Bennet, who instructed her to enjoy herself as much as possible. As they waved her off in the carriage, Elizabeth reflected that that was one piece of advice that Lydia was certain to take.

# CHAPTER SIXTEEN

Things were rather gloomy at Longbourn after the regiment left for Brighton. The house felt very quiet without Lydia and Mrs Bennet and Kitty spent a great deal of time complaining about how dull everything was.

Happily for Elizabeth, there was soon a chance to escape. Her aunt and uncle, Mr and Mrs Gardiner, invited her to accompany them on a visit to Derbyshire. Elizabeth was thrilled with the idea of exploring the wild and beautiful Derbyshire peaks, and she knew that Mrs Gardiner was especially looking forward to showing her the town of Lambton, where she had grown up.

It was July when they set off. The first part of their journey took them through Oxford, Blenheim, Warwick and Birmingham, and Elizabeth enjoyed seeing all the sights. Presently, they came to Derbyshire, and the pretty little town of Lambton.

'Did you know we are only five miles away from Pemberley – the grand house that belongs to Mr Darcy,' said Mrs Gardiner, over breakfast at the pleasant inn where they were staying. 'It's a beautiful place and I'd love to see it again. Why don't we go and visit?'

After all that had passed between herself and Mr Darcy, Elizabeth felt she had no business going to look at his house. She hurriedly told her aunt that she was tired of seeing great houses, and had no pleasure in looking at sumptuous carpets and satin curtains.

'If Pemberley was merely a fine house, richly furnished, I shouldn't care about it myself,' agreed

Mrs Gardiner. 'But the grounds are delightful – they have some of the finest woods in the country. And wouldn't you like to see a place you have heard so much about? I know Mr Darcy may not be so pleasant, but the associations are not all bad – remember, Mr Wickham spent his childhood there.'

Elizabeth said nothing but took a sip of her tea.

Mr Gardiner was asking the maid about Pemberley, and whether the family were at home for the summer. When she explained that the family were all away in London, Elizabeth felt relieved. If there was no chance of meeting Mr Darcy, perhaps it might be possible for them to visit – after all, she was rather curious to see his house for herself.

As they drove towards Pemberley later that morning, Elizabeth watched keenly for the first sight of the grounds. They drove for some time through beautiful woods, and then found themselves suddenly at the top of a sweeping hill, with a magnificent view of Pemberley House on the opposite side of the valley. It was a large, handsome building, backed by a ridge of high green hills, with a stream running before it. Elizabeth was delighted with the sight.

When they arrived at the door, they were greeted by the housekeeper, who was only too willing to show them over the house. The rooms were lofty and elegant, but what Elizabeth loved most were the glorious views from the windows of river, hills, trees and valleys.

*To think that I might have been the mistress of all this,* she thought in wonder, as she gazed out.

Meanwhile, Mr Gardiner had been chatting with the housekeeper, who had told him that Mr Darcy was expected to arrive tomorrow 'with a large party of friends'. Elizabeth breathed a sigh of relief at this narrow escape, very glad indeed that they had missed him.

Mrs Gardiner called her over to look at a picture, which Elizabeth saw at once was a miniature of Mr Wickham. 'Look – how do you like this, Lizzy?' she said with a smile.

Looking over, the housekeeper explained that

this was a picture of the son of her late master's steward. 'He's now gone into the army,' she added. 'But I'm afraid he has turned out very wild!'

Mrs Gardiner gave Elizabeth a quick sidelong glance, but the housekeeper was already pointing out another miniature. 'That is my master, Mr Darcy.'

'It is a handsome face,' said Mrs Gardiner. 'Lizzy, you can tell us whether it is like him or not.'

The housekeeper looked respectfully at Elizabeth. 'Does this young lady know Mr Darcy?'

'A little,' said Elizabeth.

'Isn't he a handsome gentleman, ma'am?'

'Yes, very handsome.'

'I'm sure I know no one so handsome, nor so kind. I've never have had a cross word from him in my life and I've known him ever since he was four years old,' said the housekeeper, with a beaming smile. 'And look – this picture is Miss Georgiana,

his sister. She is the handsomest young lady that was ever seen, and so accomplished. She plays and sings all day long. In the next room, there is a new piano that has just arrived for her – a present from her from Mr Darcy. He is always so generous, just like his father.'

'His father was certainly an excellent man,' observed Mrs Gardiner, looking rather surprised at all this praise for Mr Darcy.

'Yes, ma'am, indeed he was – and his son will be just like him, the best landlord and the best master,' said the housekeeper warmly. 'There is not one of his tenants or servants who would not speak well of him. Some people call him proud, but I think that's just because he doesn't prattle away like other young men do.'

'This fine account of Mr Darcy is quite at odds with his behaviour to Mr Wickham,' whispered Mrs Gardiner to Elizabeth.

'Perhaps we might have been deceived,' said Elizabeth quickly.

She found herself staring for some moments at the picture of Mr Darcy. He certainly did look handsome and, as usual, rather haughty. But hearing the housekeeper's praise of him had made her see him differently. Was it her imagination or was there a spark of kindness and perhaps even a little shyness in his expression, as well as pride?

She was still thinking about it as they finished their tour of the house, said farewell to the housekeeper and went out to look at the gardens. As they walked across a long, green lawn, Elizabeth turned back to take a last look at the beautiful house – and as she did so, to her enormous astonishment, Mr Darcy himself appeared from the direction of the stables.

It was so sudden that Elizabeth could not possibly avoid him. Their eyes met and Mr Darcy started in surprise at seeing her there.

'Miss Bennet!' he exclaimed.

Elizabeth's cheeks burned. This was the most unfortunate thing in the world! She hardly knew what she was saying as she stammered a reply to his polite enquiries about her health and her family. She felt overcome with shame. Oh, why had they come? How must it appear to him to see her there? If they had left the house only ten minutes sooner, they would not have seen him, for it was obvious that he had only just that moment arrived.

In spite of her embarrassment, Elizabeth couldn't help noticing that Mr Darcy seemed different. He was obviously amazed to see her – yet never before had she seen him so relaxed and easy. What a contrast to the last time they had met at Rosings Park.

'Will you do me the honour of introducing me to your friends?' he asked, looking over to where Mr and Mrs Gardiner were standing a little way across the lawn.

Elizabeth was astonished. *He must take them for people of fashion*, she thought. *He won't want to know them when he realises they are only my relations*. But once her aunt and uncle had been introduced, Mr Darcy continued to talk warmly to them, chatting to Mrs Gardiner about Lambton, and to Mr Gardiner about fishing, inviting him to fish in his trout-streams as often as he chose, and even promising to supply him with fishing tackle. At this friendliness and generosity, Mrs Gardiner gave Elizabeth a wondering look.

Presently Mr Darcy encouraged them to walk through the grounds to see some of the best fishing spots, and as they did so, Elizabeth took the opportunity to say to him quietly, 'I am so sorry we have intruded on you like this. I understood you were away. Your housekeeper told us you and your friends wouldn't be here until tomorrow.'

'That was indeed my plan,' said Mr Darcy, nodding seriously. 'But some business obliged me to come early, before everyone else. The rest of the party will join me tomorrow, and among them are Mr Bingley and his sisters.'

Elizabeth blushed. She could not help thinking of the last time Mr Bingley's name had come up in conversation between them, in the uncomfortable scene at the Parsonage.

'There is one other person in the party who particularly wishes to know you,' Mr Darcy went on, a little more shyly. 'Will you allow me to introduce my sister to you while you are staying at Lambton?'

Elizabeth was surprised but said 'yes' at once. In spite of everything that had happened, Mr Darcy obviously did not think too badly of her, if he wished to introduce her to his sister.

After Mr Darcy had shown Mr Gardiner the best fishing spots, they said their goodbyes, Mr Darcy helping the ladies into their carriage.

'Well!' exclaimed Mr Gardiner as they drove away. 'Mr Darcy is not at all what I expected. He seems perfectly well-behaved and polite.'

'There is something a little stately about him, to be sure,' agreed his wife. 'But though some people call him proud, I saw nothing of it. I really could not have thought he could have behaved in such a cruel way to anybody as he has done to poor Wickham.'

Elizabeth could only shake her head – and as the carriage drove away, she found herself staring back at Mr Darcy.

# CHAPTER SEVENTEEN

It was only a day or two later that Mr Darcy came to call on Elizabeth at the inn in Lambton – bringing with him his sister as he had promised.

Miss Darcy was a tall girl with gentle manners, and Elizabeth saw at once that she was exceedingly shy – not in the least like the proud and haughty young woman Mr Wickham had described.

They had only spoken a few words together before a quick step was heard on the stairs, and Mr Bingley appeared, beaming all over his face, obviously delighted to see Elizabeth again. 'It has been such a long time since I had the pleasure of seeing you!' he exclaimed, after the first greetings were over. 'More than eight months. We have not met since November, when we were all dancing together at Netherfield.'

He looked rather wistful at the thought, and Elizabeth couldn't help feeling it was a good sign he remembered so exactly. Although they were perfectly friendly to each other, she didn't notice any special connection between him and Miss Darcy – and although he made no particular mention of Jane, she noticed he was very quick to ask after her family. 'Are *all* your sisters still at Longbourn?' he added eagerly, looking most relieved when Elizabeth said that they were, except for Lydia, who was away in Brighton.

The visitors stayed with them for half an hour, in which Mr Darcy seemed warmer and friendlier than ever. Before they left, he and his sister invited Elizabeth and Mr and Mrs Gardiner to dine with them at Pemberley the next day – an invitation they were pleased to accept.

It was strange to return to the beautiful house once more – no longer as visitors admiring the grounds, but this time as Mr Darcy's invited guests. Sitting in an elegant salon, they found him with Miss Darcy and Mr Bingley – as well as Miss Bingley and Mrs

Hurst, neither of whom looked very happy to see Elizabeth again. In fact, Miss Bingley barely spoke to her at all, apart from a chilly enquiry after the health of her family.

Presently a meal of cold meat, cake and beautiful grapes, nectarines and peaches was served. While she ate, Elizabeth watched all that was going on around her: Miss Darcy shyly responding to Mrs

Gardiner's kindly conversation; Mr Darcy talking in the friendliest way to Mr Gardiner; and Miss Bingley smiling across at Mr Darcy in between throwing sharp, curious looks in Elizabeth's direction, as if wondering how she could possibly have come to be there.

After a while, Miss Bingley called across the room to Elizabeth. 'Pray, Miss Eliza – are the regiment now departed from Meryton? That must be a very great loss to your family. I expect you will be especially missing the company of Mr Wickham?'

At the mention of Mr Wickham's name, Mr Darcy looked up sharply, and Miss Georgiana's cheeks flushed red with sudden unhappiness. But Elizabeth managed to reply calmly, smoothing over the uncomfortable moment, and Mr Darcy gave her a grateful smile.

Later, after Elizabeth and her aunt and uncle had left, Miss Bingley began to give voice to her opinions on their guests.

'How dreadful Eliza Bennet looked today,' she said. 'I never in my life saw anyone so altered. She is grown so coarse.'

'I should hardly know her,' agreed Mrs Hurst.

'I can see little difference,' said Mr Darcy coolly. 'She is perhaps a little tanned, but that is natural given that she has been travelling in the summer.'

'I must confess I never saw much beauty in her,' Miss Bingley went on. 'Her face is too thin. Her teeth are tolerable, I suppose – but nothing out of the common way. And as for her eyes, which I have sometimes heard called *fine*, I never could see anything special about them. They have a sharp, shrewish look which I do not like.'

Mr Darcy looked irritated by this, but said nothing, and Miss Bingley went on, 'I remember how amazed we were on first meeting her to hear her described as a beauty. I particularly remember you, Mr Darcy, being astonished at the very idea.' She giggled delightedly at the memory. 'But afterwards she seemed to improve on you. I believe you thought her rather pretty at one time.'

'Yes, I did,' said Mr Darcy shortly. 'But for some time now I have considered her one of the handsomest women I know.'

He turned away, leaving Miss Bingley staring after him with a very sour expression on her face.

Meanwhile, back at the inn, Mrs Gardiner and Elizabeth talked over their visit to Pemberley. They discussed Mr Darcy's sister, his friends, and his house – everything but Mr Darcy himself, though Elizabeth was longing to know what her aunt thought of him. As for Mrs Gardiner, she was becoming more and more curious about the relationship between Mr Darcy and her niece.

# CHAPTER EIGHTEEN

For several days, Elizabeth had been waiting for a letter from Jane – and to her delight, the very next morning, two arrived at once. Her aunt and uncle were out for a walk, so Elizabeth settled down to read them alone, eager to hear the news.

The first letter was dated five days ago. The first part of the letter was quite ordinary, relating all that had been happening at Longbourn – but then, Elizabeth read:

*Since writing the above, something has happened of an unexpected and serious nature. But I am afraid of alarming you: we are all quite well. What I have to say relates to poor Lydia.*

*A message arrived at twelve o'clock last night, after we had all gone to bed. It came from Colonel Forster, who informed us that Lydia had run away to Scotland to be married to one of his officers – in fact, to Mr Wickham!*

*I am very, very sorry. It is such an imprudent marriage. But I am willing to hope for the best and that his character has been misunderstood. At least he is not marrying her out of greed, for he must know that our father has no money to give her. Our poor mother is very unhappy; how thankful I am that we never let her know what has been said against Mr Wickham.*

Elizabeth instantly seized Jane's second letter and tore it open. She saw it had been written the following day.

*Dearest Lizzy, I hardly know what to write, but*

*I have bad news for you. Unfortunate as a marriage between Mr Wickham and Lydia would be, what is worse is that it seems that <u>it may not have taken place at all</u>. Though a note she left for Mrs Forster said they had gone to Scotland to be married, it now seems that Wickham never had any intention of marrying Lydia.*

*Colonel Forster has managed to trace them as far as London. He shook his head when I expressed hopes that they might have planned to marry there instead, and said he feared Wickham was not a man to be trusted.*

*Everyone is terribly upset. Our mother is very ill and keeps to her room, and as for our father, I never in my life saw him so affected. Dearest Lizzy, I hope you will come home as soon as possible. Our father is going to London with Colonel Forster to try and find Lydia, and our uncle's assistance would be a world of help to them.*

'Oh!' cried Elizabeth aloud, darting up from her seat the moment she finished reading Jane's letter. But as she came towards the door it opened suddenly, and Mr Darcy appeared before her. He stared at her pale face, but before he could say anything, she exclaimed, 'I beg your pardon, but I must find Mr Gardiner this moment – I have not an instant to lose!'

'What's the matter?' he asked. 'You must let me or the maid go instead. You are not well – you cannot go.'

Elizabeth hesitated, but she agreed; the maid was summoned and was asked to fetch Mr and Mrs Gardiner.

Once the maid had hurried off, Mr Darcy spoke to her gently. 'Sit down and let me fetch you a glass of wine to help you recover.'

'No thank you,' said Elizabeth, trying to compose herself. 'There is nothing wrong with me. I am quite well. I am only distressed by some dreadful news which I have just received from Longbourn. It is no good trying to conceal it. My youngest sister Lydia has run away and has thrown herself into the power of *Mr Wickham*. You know him too well to doubt the rest. And to think that I could have prevented this, if I had told my family what I knew about him! But now it is too late.'

'I am grieved indeed,' said Mr Darcy gravely. 'Grieved and shocked. But is it absolutely certain?' 'Oh yes. They left Brighton together and were traced as far as London.'

'Has there been an attempt to find her?'

'My father has gone to London to look for her, and Jane has written to ask for my uncle's help. I hope we will be on our way in half an hour. But however will anyone be able to find them?'

Mr Darcy had begun walking up and down the room, frowning heavily. After a few moments he said, 'I imagine that all this will prevent us having the pleasure of seeing you at Pemberley today.'

'Oh yes. Be so kind as to apologise for us to Miss Darcy. Say that urgent business calls us home. Keep the truth a secret for a while, if you can.'

He promised he would, said he was very sorry once again, and gave her a serious nod before he departed.

A minute or two later, Mr and Mrs Gardiner

returned. Elizabeth poured out the story and showed them Jane's letters, and an hour later, they were packed and hurrying into the carriage.

The road home took them alongside the grounds of Pemberley. As she took one long last look at the beautiful woods passing them by, Elizabeth felt quite certain that she was leaving Mr Darcy behind her for good.

On their journey back to Longbourn, Elizabeth and her aunt and uncle could talk of nothing but Lydia and Mr Wickham. At first, Mr Gardiner suggested that perhaps Mr Wickham really had fallen in love with Lydia and wanted to marry her, but Elizabeth shook her head.

'I don't believe it,' she said. 'Mr Wickham will never marry a woman without money – and he must know that Lydia has none. Besides, he is false and deceitful.'

'How can you be so sure?' asked Mrs Gardiner in surprise.

Elizabeth quickly explained a little of what Mr Darcy had told her of Mr Wickham. 'Of course, I never told Lydia any of this,' she finished miserably. 'If only I had!'

'You had no reason to suspect that she was fond of Mr Wickham?' asked Mrs Gardiner.

'No, not in the slightest. When he first came to Meryton she admired him, but so did all the girls. He never paid her any special attention, and there were others amongst the officers who seemed to be her favourites.'

'Don't worry, Lizzy,' said Mr Gardiner reassuringly. 'I'll follow your father to London, and we'll do everything we can to find her.'

The journey back home seemed to pass very slowly, but at long last, the carriage came up the drive towards Longbourn, where Jane came running out to meet them.

'Is there any news?' asked Elizabeth, as she hugged her sister.

'Not yet,' said Jane. 'Father has gone to town – and now our uncle is here to help him, I hope all will be well.'

They all hurried upstairs to Mrs Bennet's room at once. She greeted them with a mixture of tears, angry exclamations at the villainous behaviour of Mr Wickham and many complaints about her nerves.

'If we had all gone to Brighton, this would never have happened,' she wailed into her handkerchief. 'My poor dear Lydia had no one to take care of her! I am sure the Forsters must have neglected her, for she is not the kind of girl to do such a thing, if she was well looked after. Poor dear child! And now Mr Bennet has gone away, and I know he will fight Wickham, and then he will be killed – and then what is to become of us all? The Collinses will turn us out of the house before he is cold in his grave . . . and if you are not kind to us, brother, I do not know what we shall do!' she finished fretfully.

Mr Gardiner patted her hand and tried to console her, promising that he would go to London the very next day to help Mr Bennet find Lydia.

'My dear brother! That is exactly what I would like. And when you get to town and find them, if they are not already married you must *make* them marry. And above all things, keep Mr Bennet from fighting. Tell him what a dreadful state I am in – that I am frightened out of my wits, and have such tremblings, such flutterings all over me, such spasms in my side and pains in my head, and such beatings at my heart that I can get no rest night or day. And tell Lydia not to give any directions about wedding clothes until she has seen me, for she does not know which are the best places to buy them!' she added.

She went on like this until dinner time, when

they left her to continue to vent her feelings to the housekeeper, while they all went down to the dining room.

'This is a most unfortunate affair and will probably be much talked of,' Mary observed primly as they ate.

'Well *I* don't see that Lydia has done anything so very dreadful,' said Kitty. 'She and Wickham had fallen in love. I think running away together to be married is romantic.'

'Not so romantic if Wickham never really planned to marry her and is only amusing himself at Lydia's expense,' said Elizabeth. She turned to Jane. 'What did Colonel Forster say? Had he no idea at all?'

'He did admit that he had suspected some feelings on Lydia's side,' said Jane. 'But nothing to give him any alarm.'

'What about the letter she left for Mrs Forster? What did it say?'

'I have it here,' said Jane, and handed Elizabeth a scribbled note.

*My dear Harriet,*

*You will laugh when you know where I am gone and I cannot help laughing myself at your surprise tomorrow morning when I am missed. I have gone to Scotland to be married and if you cannot guess with who, I will think you a simpleton – for there is only one man in the world I love!*

*Don't send them word at Longbourn – it will make the surprise all the greater when I write to them and sign my name <u>Lydia Wickham</u>. What a good joke it will be! I can hardly write for laughing!*

*Your friend,*

*Lydia Bennet*

'Obviously she really believed they were going to get married,' said Jane.

But Elizabeth just sighed and put down her

knife and fork, feeling she had no appetite for dinner. Lydia might think that running away with Mr Wickham was a good joke – but the joke would be on her if the wedding did not take place. Now that she had gone away with him, no other respectable man would consider marrying her. She would have to stay at home with her parents for ever, her reputation quite ruined. Marriage to the dastardly Mr Wickham was Lydia's only hope.

# CHAPTER NINETEEN

While they waited for any news of Lydia, the days at Longbourn seemed to pass by very slowly. Mr and Mrs Gardiner had gone back to London, and although their aunt, Mrs Phillips, visited them regularly to try and cheer them all up, she never came without bringing some new story of Wickham's wickedness. All at once, everyone in Meryton seemed to have a tale to tell about the man who – just a few months ago – they had all thought perfectly charming and delightful. Now he was said to owe money to every shopkeeper in town, and to have been involved in all kinds of shocking intrigues, scandals and seductions.

Everyone agreed he was the most dreadful young man in the world. Although she did not believe all of these tall tales, they did not do much to improve Elizabeth's spirits, and even Jane, who always thought the best of everyone, became rather gloomy.

Each day they waited anxiously for the post to arrive in case there was any news from London. But before they heard anything more of Lydia, a letter arrived from Mr Collins. It was addressed to Mr Bennet, but as he had told her to read any letters that came while he was away, Elizabeth opened it at once.

*I feel called upon by our relationship and my profession to condole with you about your situation. Be assured, my dear sir, that Mrs Collins and I sympathise with you in your distress – which must be of the <u>bitterest kind</u>. And it is the more to be lamented because, my dear Charlotte informs me,* *your daughter's behaviour is the result of <u>great</u> <u>indulgence</u>! Though at the same time I am inclined to think that her disposition must be <u>naturally</u> <u>bad</u>.*

*In any case, you are most <u>grievously</u> to be pitied – an opinion which is shared by Mrs Collins, Lady Catherine and her daughter, to whom I have related the affair in full. They agree with me that such behaviour in one daughter will certainly injure the fortunes of all the others. For who, as Lady Catherine herself says, will connect themselves with such a family?*

*With this in mind, let me advise you, dear sir, to throw off your unworthy child, and leave her to face the consequences of what she has done.*

'Dreadful man!' exclaimed Elizabeth – but she was soon distracted by a short note that had arrived from Mr Gardiner. He wrote that they had not yet found any trace of Lydia in London, but that

Colonel Forster had discovered that Mr Wickham had left over a thousand pounds of gambling debts behind him in Brighton.

'He is a gambler too?' said Jane. 'How shocking!'

The letter also said that Mr Bennet would shortly return home to his family, while Mr Gardiner continued the search for Lydia alone. This did not please Mrs Bennet at all.

'He is coming home without poor Lydia? But who is to fight Wickham and make him marry her if he comes away?'

Two days later, Mr Bennet arrived back at Longbourn. He said little but looked very grave and serious indeed.

'You must not be too severe upon yourself,' said Elizabeth, trying to comfort him.

'No, Lizzy, let me once in my life feel how much I have been to blame,' said Mr Bennet gloomily. 'You were quite right: I should never have permitted Lydia to go to Brighton.'

'Do you think they are still in London?' asked Jane.

'I am sure of it. Where else can they be so well hidden?'

'And Lydia always wanted to go to London,' recalled Kitty.

'Well, she is happy then, perhaps,' said their father with a sigh.

Jane got up to take Mrs Bennet some tea. 'She still keeps to her room, does she?' asked Mr Bennet. 'Very good – it gives such elegance to our misfortune. Perhaps I shall do the same: I will sit in my library in my nightcap and dressing gown and give as much trouble as I can, until Kitty runs away.'

'*I* am not going to run away Papa,' said Kitty at once. 'If I should ever go to Brighton, I would behave better than Lydia.'

'You, go to Brighton? I wouldn't trust you as

near it as Eastbourne, not for fifty pounds!' said Mr Bennet. 'No, Kitty, I have at last learned to be cautious – and you shall feel the effects of it. No officer is ever to enter my house again. Balls will be absolutely forbidden. And you are never to stir out of doors until you can prove that you have spent ten minutes of every day in a sensible manner!'

Kitty, who took all these threats quite seriously, began to cry. 'Well, well,' said Mr Bennet, patting her shoulder. 'Do not make yourself unhappy. If you are good girl for ten years, perhaps I'll reconsider after that.'

Two days after Mr Bennet's return, a letter came for him from Mr Gardiner. Hearing the news that a message had arrived, Jane and Elizabeth came running out into the garden, where their father was walking up and down examining the letter, a worried frown upon his face.

'Oh, Papa, what news does it bring – good or

bad?' asked Elizabeth, who was more in the habit of running and so reached her father first.

'Read it aloud,' said her father, handing her the letter as Jane came panting up behind her. 'I hardly know what to make of it.'

*At last I am able to send you some tidings of my niece and Mr Wickham. I have located them and seen them both. They are not married, but if you are willing to carry out the arrangements which I have made on your behalf, I hope it will not be long before they are.*

*All that is required of you is to ensure your daughter her equal share of the five thousand pounds your children will inherit after your death, and during your life to give her one hundred pounds a year.*

*You will be glad to hear that Mr Wickham's circumstances are not quite so hopeless as they are generally believed to be. Colonel Forster will pay off his debts in Brighton, and I ask you to do the same in Meryton — I enclose a list.*

*There is no need for you to come to town — stay quietly at Longbourn, and I will take care of everything.*

'Then perhaps Wickham is not as undeserving as we thought,' said Jane hopefully. 'Perhaps he really does love Lydia?'

But Elizabeth was not so sure, and Mr Bennet looked very grave indeed. 'There are two things I want very much to know,' he said slowly. 'One is how much your uncle has paid Mr Wickham to bring this marriage about. And the other is how am I ever going to repay him?'

'Why, what do you mean?' cried Jane at once.

'From all we now know of him, I am sure Wickham would never have agreed to marry Lydia for only one hundred pounds a year,' explained Mr Bennet. 'In fact, I would be surprised if he accepted anything less than a dowry of ten thousand pounds.'

'*Ten thousand pounds*?' repeated Elizabeth in amazement.

'How could our uncle possibly spare so much money?' wondered Jane.

But to that Mr Bennet had no answer. He went back to the library to write his reply to Mr Gardiner, his face clouded over with worry.

The letter had quite a different effect on Mrs Bennet. The moment she learned that Lydia would soon be married, her joy burst forth. 'Oh my dear, dear Lydia! And my good, kind brother! I knew he would manage everything. How I long to see her – and dear Wickham too, of course.'

Jane tried to explain about Mr Gardiner, and the money he must have paid Wickham to bring the marriage about, but Mrs Bennet shrugged this off at once. 'Well, who else should do that but her own uncle? I am so happy! A daughter married. And she only just sixteen! But the wedding clothes – I will write to Mrs Gardiner about them. Lizzy, run down and ask your father how much money he will give her. No, stay, I will go myself. My dear, dear Lydia! *Mrs Wickham* – how well it sounds. And how merry we shall be together when we meet.'

She bounced up from her bed where she had been languishing ever since the news of Lydia running away had first arrived. 'I will go to Meryton as soon as I am dressed and tell the good news to my sister. And I will call on Lady Lucas too,' she announced. 'Kitty, run down and order the carriage at once. And the servants shall have a bowl of punch to celebrate.'

Elizabeth gave Jane an exasperated glance. It was a great relief that her uncle had managed to arrange for Lydia's wedding – but she felt certain that there was nothing at all to celebrate about Mr Wickham becoming part of the family.

# CHAPTER TWENTY

Thanks to Mrs Bennet's busy tongue, the news of Lydia's marriage soon spread throughout the neighbourhood. The spiteful old ladies of Meryton raised their eyebrows and tutted over the idea of such a disreputable husband, but Mrs Bennet didn't notice. She was in a delighted mood. She had been dreaming about having a daughter married for years – and now, at last, it was actually going to happen. She talked of nothing but fine wedding clothes, new carriages, servants and suitable houses for the newly married pair.

'Haye Park might do,' she pondered over breakfast. 'If the Gouldings would leave. Or the great house of Stoke, if the drawing room were larger. But then, it is so far off – I could not bear to have Lydia ten miles away. And as for Purvis Lodge, the attics there are dreadful.'

But another letter from Mr Gardiner soon disappointed all her plans. He wrote that Mr Wickham was to leave Colonel Forster's regiment and join another regiment in the north of England.

'But why should Lydia go so far away? And be taken away from the regiment where she knows everyone?' Mrs Bennet complained. 'She is so fond of Mrs Forster, and there are several of the young men there that she likes very much. This new regiment may not be so pleasant.'

'Can't you see that Lydia and Mr Wickham need to make a fresh start away from all the gossip and scandal they have caused?' asked Elizabeth impatiently, but Mrs Bennet paid her no attention. She was already distracted by the next part of the letter, in which Mr Gardiner wrote that Lydia and her new husband would like to pay a visit to Longbourn on their journey north.

Several days later, a carriage was seen approaching the house, with Lydia leaning excitedly from the window. The family assembled in the breakfast room to greet them: Mrs Bennet beaming with delight, Elizabeth and her sisters uneasy, and Mr Bennet looking very sombre indeed.

Soon Lydia's voice was heard in the hall, the door was flung open, and she ran into the room with Wickham following more sedately behind her. Mrs Bennet welcomed them both rapturously.

Elizabeth saw at once that Lydia was exactly her usual self: wild, noisy, and not in the least ashamed of all the trouble she had caused. In fact, she seemed delighted with herself, turning from one sister to another, demanding their congratulations on her marriage. As for Mr Wickham, he too was perfectly easy and relaxed, as though he had done nothing wrong.

'Just think, it is only three months since I went away! I had no idea that I would be married when I came back again – although I thought it would be very good fun if I was,' Lydia prattled. 'Oh, Mama! Do our neighbours know I am married? When we

came through Meryton I let down the window and took off my glove so everyone might see my ring, and waved and smiled like anything.'

As they passed into the dining room, Lydia pushed herself in front of Jane and took the seat at Mrs Bennet's right hand. 'I take your place at the table now,' she told Jane smugly. 'You must sit lower down – because *I* am a married woman – even though I am the youngest of you all!'

Lydia and Mr Wickham stayed at Longbourn for two weeks, and Elizabeth and her sisters grew heartily sick of hearing Lydia's praise for her 'dear Wickham'.

'Isn't my husband charming?' she demanded of Jane and Elizabeth. 'Isn't he handsome? I am sure you must envy me. I only hope you will have half my good luck. You should go to Brighton – that is the place to find husbands. Or perhaps you can come and stay with me in our new home, and I am sure I shall get husbands for you both before the winter is over.'

'Thank you for my share of the favour,' said Elizabeth drily. 'But I don't particularly like your way of getting husbands.'

Seeming not to have heard her, Lydia went on. 'Lizzy, I haven't yet given *you* an account of my wedding. You really must hear all about it. I was terrifically excited of course. My aunt was there all the time I was dressing, talking away as though she was giving a sermon, but I barely heard a word, I was so thrilled. Then she and my uncle came with me to the church, and Wickham arrived with Mr Darcy and—'

'*Mr Darcy*?' interrupted Elizabeth in sudden amazement. 'Whatever was Mr Darcy doing there?'

'Gracious me, I quite forgot! I ought not to have said a word about it. I promised faithfully – what will Wickham say? It was to be such a secret,' giggled

Lydia. 'You must not ask me any questions for if I tell you anything more Wickham will be angry.'

Mr Darcy had been at Lydia and Wickham's wedding? Elizabeth could scarcely imagine anything that seemed more unlikely. She said nothing more to Lydia, but she could not rest until she had written a letter to her aunt to ask how he, of all people, should have been there.

She had a letter back from Mrs Gardiner shortly afterwards, and she hurried out into the garden to read it:

*I was surprised to receive your letter, but if you do not know the part Mr Darcy played in arranging Lydia's wedding, I will relate it to you now.*

*The day after your father returned to Longbourn, we had an unexpected visit from Mr Darcy. He told us that he had managed to find out where Lydia and Mr Wickham were staying, and he had seen them both. He had left Derbyshire only the day after we did, and had travelled to London in order to find them. He told us that he felt what had happened was his own fault, as he had been too proud to make his private business known to the world.*

*When Mr Darcy discovered that Wickham had no intention of marrying Lydia, he persuaded him to do so – paying his debts and finding a place for him with a new regiment. He made all the arrangements for the wedding – nothing was to be done that he did not do himself, and your uncle, instead of being allowed to be of use to Lydia, was forced to take credit for it all.*

*Will you be angry with me, my dear Lizzy, if I take the opportunity to say how very much I like Mr Darcy? His behaviour to us through all this was as generous and kind as it was in Derbyshire. In my opinion, he needs only a little liveliness – and if he marries the right person, perhaps his wife will teach him that?*

Elizabeth frowned over these final sentences, but before she had chance to think very much about them, Mr Wickham came strolling out into the garden, looking very pleased with himself. She quickly folded the letter and tucked it away in her pocket.

'I am afraid I am interrupting your solitary walk, my dear sister,' he said, flashing her with his charming smile. 'But I hope I am not unwelcome? We were always good friends, after all.'

Elizabeth nodded politely but said nothing.

'I hear that you have been to visit Pemberley?' Mr Wickham went on. 'I should so much like to see it again myself one day,' he added, with a wistful sigh. 'Did you happen to see Mr Darcy while you were there? I understand from Mr and Mrs Gardiner that you had.'

'Yes, he introduced us to his sister,' Elizabeth replied briefly.

'And did you like her?'

'Very much.'

'Well, I have heard that she has improved

within the past year or two,' said Wickham airily.
'When I last saw her she was not very promising.
Tell me, did you go by the village of Kympton
while you were in the area?'

'I don't think we did.'

'I only mention it because that is where I ought
to have been parson, you know. A delightful place.
It should have suited me perfectly.'

'How would you have liked giving sermons?'

'Exceedingly well. The peace and quiet of such
a life would have been perfect happiness to me.'

'I've heard that there was a time when it was
not so appealing to you as it seems to be at present
– and that in fact you turned down the opportunity,'
said Elizabeth sharply.

Mr Wickham looked uncomfortable and only
said, 'Well – er – I . . .'

There was a moment's awkward pause, and
then Elizabeth gave him a quick, charming smile
of her own. 'Come, Mr Wickham, we are

brother and sister now. Let's not quarrel about the past.'

No one except Mrs Bennet seemed very sorry to say goodbye when the time came for Mr and Mrs Wickham to depart.

'My dear Lydia!' Mrs Bennet wept. 'When shall we meet again?'

'Oh, I don't know. Not for two or three years perhaps,' said Lydia casually.

'You must write to me very often, my dear!'

'I will when I can. But we married women don't have much time for writing. Of course, my sisters may write to me. They will have nothing better to do.'

Mr Wickham smiled and bowed in his most gallant manner, bidding them all *adieu*.

'What a fine fellow,' said Mr Bennet with a sarcastic smirk, once the carriage had at last gone, leaving Mrs Bennet sniffing into her handkerchief.

'He simpers and smiles at us all. I am tremendously proud of him, you know. Even Sir William Lucas can't boast of such a son-in-law!'

# CHAPTER TWENTY-ONE

No sooner had Lydia and Mr Wickham left Longbourn than Mrs Phillips arrived with the latest news from Meryton. 'Have you heard? Mr Bingley is coming back to Netherfield at last,' she twittered, almost before she had taken off her bonnet.

Elizabeth glanced over at Jane at once, but Jane looked quite calm, as though this information did not affect her in the slightest. However, Elizabeth knew her sister much too well to believe that was true.

On the other hand, Mrs Bennet was obviously thrilled by the news that Mr Bingley was returning to the neighbourhood. 'As soon as he is back at

Netherfield, you *must* visit him,' she instructed her husband.

'No, no,' said Mr Bennet from behind his book. 'You told me last year that if I visited him, he would marry one of my daughters. But it all ended in nothing – and I won't be sent on a fool's errand again.'

But as it happened, Mr Bennet did not have to call on Mr Bingley, for Mr Bingley came to visit Longbourn only a few days later. Mrs Bennet saw him riding towards the house on his glossy black horse and was in a great fever of excitement at once.

'Look – there's a gentleman with him,' said Kitty, who was peering out of the drawing-room window beside her. 'It looks like that man who used to be with him before. What's his name? You know, that tall, proud one.'

'Mr Darcy! Well, any friend of Mr Bingley's will always be welcome here – though I must say I hate the very sight of him,' Mrs Bennet said with a tut.

Jane and Elizabeth exchanged glances. Mrs Bennet had no idea how much they all owed to Mr Darcy – after all, he was the one who had secretly made all the arrangements for Lydia's marriage. Elizabeth felt more and more awkward as Mrs Bennet went on complaining about Mr Darcy, even as they heard the sound of horses' hooves coming up to the house.

As the two gentlemen came into the room, Elizabeth fixed her attention on her sewing, trying to look as though everything was perfectly ordinary. She saw at once that Mr Darcy appeared stiff and serious – much more like the man she had first met in the ballroom at Meryton than the kindly and pleasant host he had been in Derbyshire.

As for Mr Bingley, his cheeks were pinker than ever, and he looked both pleased and embarrassed as Mrs Bennet gave him a warm welcome. Elizabeth winced as she saw what a cold, short greeting Mrs

Bennet gave to Mr Darcy, before turning back to beam at Mr Bingley once more.

'It is such a long time since you went away! We began to fear you would never come back again. People did say you meant to give up Netherfield entirely, but I hope that is not true?' she began. 'A great many changes have taken place since you went away. Miss Lucas is married – and so is one of my own daughters. You may have seen it in the papers, only they did not put it in right. It only said *"Lately, George Wickham Esq to Miss Lydia Bennet"* without a word about who her father is or where she lives or anything. Now they are gone away north where Mr Wickham is to join a new regiment. Thank heavens he has *some* friends to help him – though perhaps not as many as he deserves,' she added, with a glower in Mr Darcy's direction.

Elizabeth could not have felt more embarrassed. She stared down at her sewing and longed for the gentlemen to depart. When at last they had gone, she and Jane escaped the drawing room to talk in private.

'Now that this first meeting with Mr Bingley is over, I feel perfectly calm,' Jane declared. 'It is as though we are just indifferent acquaintances and nothing more.'

But Elizabeth did not think that either Jane or Mr Bingley were at all indifferent to each other. 'Jane, take care . . .' she warned her sister.

'My dear Lizzy, you cannot think I could be in any danger now?'

Elizabeth thought of how she had seen Mr Bingley smiling adoringly in Jane's direction, even while he pretended to listen to Mrs Bennet's chatter. 'Oh, I think you are in very great danger of making him as much in love with you as ever.'

But whilst it was perfectly easy for Elizabeth to

interpret Mr Bingley's blushes and smiles, Mr Darcy remained a mystery.

Elizabeth was not the only one to guess that Mr Bingley still had feelings for Jane. Mrs Bennet had noticed it at once and was determined to seize any opportunity for the two of them to spend time together. Over the next few days she invited Mr Bingley to join them for dinner, for afternoon tea, for supper, and even for a shooting excursion with Mr Bennet. On each visit, he spent more and more time with Jane, and Elizabeth began to see her sister looking happy again.

One morning he called unexpectedly, sending Mrs Bennet into a frenzy. It was so early that no one had finished dressing, and she came running into Jane's room in her dressing gown, her hair still only half-done.

'Jane! Hurry down – Mr Bingley is here! Make haste, make haste!' she urged.

'I'll be down as soon as I can,' said Jane calmly. 'Let Kitty go down first, she's almost ready.'

'Oh, hang Kitty! What has she to do with it? Come, be quick, be quick!'

As soon as they were down in the drawing room, Mrs Bennet began to plot to give Jane and Mr Bingley an opportunity to be alone together. Mary was practising the piano, and Mr Bennet was in his library, but Kitty and Elizabeth were in the drawing room, and now she began glancing at them and winking meaningfully.

After a few minutes of this, Kitty spoke up, confused. 'What is the matter, Mama? Why do you keep winking at me? What am I to do!'

'Nothing, child,' said Mrs Bennet in a great hurry. 'I did not wink at you! Why should I wink at you? But now that you mention it, I *do* want to speak to you. Come with me.' And with that she bustled Kitty out of the room.

A few minutes later, her voice was heard outside

the drawing-room door. 'Lizzy, my dear, I want to speak to you!'

Elizabeth and Jane exchanged a quick embarrassed glance. Mrs Bennet could not have been more obvious if she had tried! But Elizabeth had no choice but to go.

'We must leave them by themselves,' her mother hissed as soon as she was in the hall. 'Come on – Kitty and I are going to sit in my dressing room.' Though Elizabeth thought that her mother looked as if she would much rather stay and listen at the door.

A short while later, Elizabeth returned to the drawing room.

The moment she opened the door, she realised that Mrs Bennet's scheming had been a success. Jane and Mr Bingley were standing close together before the fireplace, smiling delightedly at each other.

As soon as Elizabeth entered the room, they jumped apart; Bingley whispered a few words to Jane, and then hurried out of the room, his cheeks pinker than ever.

The moment he had gone, Jane flung her arms around her sister. 'I am the happiest creature in the world!' she exclaimed. 'It is too much! I don't deserve it – oh, why isn't everybody as happy as me?'

Elizabeth could not have been more delighted for Jane. After everything that had happened, after all the months of sorrow, at last she was to marry Mr Bingley.

'He says he loved me all the time. He didn't even know I was in London.' Jane smiled. 'I must go and tell Mama. He has gone to talk to Papa already. Oh, Lizzy! To think of the joy this will bring to all my dear family!'

It was a wonderful day. Jane glowed with happiness and Mr Bingley with pride. Mary was already thinking of all the books in the library at Netherfield Park and the marvellous piano, whilst Kitty dreamed of the balls that Jane could host there. Elizabeth smiled to see her beloved sister so happy, and as for Mrs Bennet, she could not have been more joyful. She forgot all about Lydia and Mr Wickham in her excitement at Jane's wonderful news.

Even Mr Bennet was satisfied. 'Jane, I congratulate you,' he said, after Mr Bingley had at last departed late that evening. 'You and Mr Bingley will do extremely well together. You are both so complying that nothing will ever be agreed on, so easy-going that every servant will cheat you, and so generous that you will always exceed your income!'

'Exceed their income? My dear Mr Bennet,'

cried Mrs Bennet, 'What are you thinking? Don't you remember that Mr Bingley has *five thousand pounds a year*! Oh, my dear, dear Jane. I was sure you could not be so beautiful for nothing! He is the handsomest young man that ever was seen.'

At last, Jane and Elizabeth were by themselves once more. 'If I could only see *you* as happy,' said Jane with a sigh. 'If there were only such another man for you!'

'If you were to give me forty such men, I should never be so happy as you,' said Elizabeth with a smile. 'Until I have your goodness, I can never have your happiness. But perhaps if I have very, *very* good luck . . . I may in time meet with another Mr Collins!'

# CHAPTER TWENTY-TWO

The news of Jane and Mr Bingley's engagement quickly spread around Meryton. Mrs Bennet wasted no time in letting everyone in the neighbourhood know, and the Bennets were soon being spoken of as the luckiest family in the world – although just a few weeks before when Lydia had run away, they had been considered the most unfortunate.

Mr Bingley visited Longbourn almost every day, and already felt like one of the family; so when, one morning, a carriage was heard driving towards the house, they all assumed it must be him. But when their visitor was announced, Elizabeth saw to her amazement that it was the last person she would ever have expected to call on her at home. It was none other than Lady Catherine de Bourgh.

She entered the room in her haughtiest manner and made no reply to Elizabeth's startled greeting except for a slight nod of the head. She sat down without saying a word, but after a few moments, she said stiffly to Elizabeth, '*That* lady, I suppose, is your mother.'

'Yes: Mama, this is Lady Catherine de Bourgh.'

'And *that*, I suppose, is one of your sisters,' she added, nodding towards Kitty.

'Yes, madam,' said Mrs Bennet hurriedly. 'She is my youngest girl but one. My youngest of all is lately married.'

Lady Catherine sniffed and looked out of the window. 'You have a very small park here,' she observed after a short silence.

'It is nothing in comparison to Rosings, my lady, I daresay — but it is much larger than Sir

William Lucas's,' Mrs Bennet couldn't resist saying.

'This must be a most inconvenient sitting room for the evening in summer. The windows face full west.'

Mrs Bennet assured her that they never sat there after dinner, and offered her some refreshments – but Lady Catherine, rather rudely, refused. Rising to her feet, she said coldly to Elizabeth, 'Miss Bennet, there seems to be a prettyish kind of little wilderness on one side of your lawn. I should be glad to take a turn in it, if you will favour me with your company.'

'Go, my dear, and show Her Ladyship the different walks,' urged Mrs Bennet eagerly.

Once outside, they proceeded in silence along the path, Lady Catherine looking more and more disagreeable by the minute. Looking at her pursed-up expression, Elizabeth wondered how she could ever have thought Lady Catherine and Mr Darcy were alike.

'You can be at no loss to understand the reason for my coming here,' said Lady Catherine abruptly.

Elizabeth was astonished: she had not the least idea what could have brought Lady Catherine to Longbourn. 'I'm afraid I don't,' she admitted.

'Miss Bennet,' said Lady Catherine in an angry tone. 'You ought to know that I am not to be trifled with! But however insincere you may choose to be, *I* am always honest and frank. I will be perfectly clear: two days ago, a most alarming report reached me. I was told that not only was your sister on the point of making a most fortunate marriage, but that *you,* Miss Elizabeth Bennet, would soon afterwards be married to my nephew – my own nephew – Mr Darcy!' Lady Catherine did not wait for any reply to this, but went on: 'I know it must be impossible – a scandalous lie.'

'If you believed it to be impossible, I am surprised you took the trouble of coming all this way to

confront me about it,' replied Elizabeth.

'I insist on having this report immediately contradicted,' Lady Catherine said, with an angry flourish of her parasol. 'Miss Bennet, has my nephew made you an offer of marriage?'

'Your Ladyship has already declared it to be impossible.'

'It ought to be so. But you may have tricked him. You may have *drawn him in*!'

'If I had, I would surely be the last person to admit it.'

'I am not accustomed to this kind of treatment! I am almost the nearest relation he has – and entitled to know all of his concerns.'

'But you are not entitled to know *mine*, nor will behaving like this encourage me to share them with you,' Elizabeth retorted at once.

'Let me be understood. This marriage can never take place. Mr Darcy is to marry *my daughter*. There – what have you to say to that?'

'Only that if he is, you can have no reason to suppose he will propose to me.'

'From their childhood they have been destined for each other. While in their cradles, his mother and I planned their marriage. And now, for all our plans to be prevented by a young woman of no importance in the world! You would be a disgrace to our family. Your name would never even be mentioned by any of us.'

'These are heavy misfortunes,' said Elizabeth sarcastically.

'Obstinate, headstrong girl!' Lady Catherine made another angry jab at the ground with her parasol. 'This is not to be endured. My daughter and my nephew are going to be married – they will not be divided by an upstart young woman without family, connections or fortune. And what of your youngest sister? I know all about her running away with Mr Wickham. Is such a girl to be my nephew's sister?' She glared at Elizabeth. 'Are the shades of

Pemberley to be thus polluted—'

But Elizabeth cut her off. 'You can have nothing else to say,' she insisted. 'You have already insulted me and my family in every possible way. I'm going back to the house.'

Lady Catherine followed her, brandishing her parasol. 'Unfeeling, selfish girl – I am ashamed of you. You are determined to ruin him!'

Elizabeth was not listening. She kept on walking.

Lady Catherine's carriage was waiting outside the house. Now she clambered inside it, and then leaned out of the window. 'I take no leave of you, Miss Bennet!' she cried out. 'I send no compliments to your mother! You deserve no such attention.' She gave Elizabeth one last glare. 'I am most seriously displeased!'

As the carriage drew away, Elizabeth stared after it, breathless with anger. But she also felt astonished.

She could scarcely believe that Lady Catherine had taken the trouble of travelling all the way from Rosings, simply to insist that she should not marry Mr Darcy. How had she even got the idea that there might be an engagement? Elizabeth had told no one but Jane of Mr Darcy's proposal – and she couldn't imagine that Mr Darcy would have spoken about it to anyone else, certainly not his aunt.

She didn't tell anyone else what Lady Catherine had said to her, not even Jane. The whole encounter had left her feeling most peculiar, and she was still feeling strange the next morning, when Mr Bennet came out of the library, looking amused and brandishing a letter in his hand.

'Lizzy, come and listen to this,' he said, beckoning her inside. 'I've received a letter from Mr Collins this morning which has surprised me greatly. I did not know before that I had *two* daughters who were about to be married – let me congratulate you!' He grinned, evidently considering his letter to be a great joke. 'He begins by offering his congratulations on Jane's engagement – I'll spare you from hearing what he has to say about that. Then he goes on to say: "*Your daughter Elizabeth, I understand, is also to be married, and her chosen partner may be reasonably considered one of the most illustrious personages in the land*". Can you possibly guess, Lizzy, who he means?'

Elizabeth felt her cheeks turning hot, as her father kept on reading. ' "*However, I must warn you that his aunt, Lady Catherine de Bourgh, does not look on the match with a friendly eye.*" ' Mr Bennet laughed. 'Mr Darcy, you see, is the man! Now, Lizzy, are you not amused by the very idea? But you don't look as though you enjoyed it – that's not like you at all.'

'Oh no, it's very amusing,' said Elizabeth uncomfortably. 'But it is so strange.'

'It certainly is. Delightfully absurd! Do you know, I would not give up Mr Collins's correspondence for anything. It's always amusing. I suppose this is why Lady Catherine came to call the other day – to refuse her consent?' Mr Bennet added with a gleeful chuckle.

Elizabeth laughed too – though the truth was, she did not feel very much like laughing at all.

# CHAPTER TWENTY-THREE

The next few days passed very much as usual: Mr Bingley came to see them almost every day, and Mrs Bennet could talk of nothing else but plans for Jane's wedding. But a week or so after Lady Catherine's visit, when Mr Bingley arrived, Elizabeth saw that he had once again brought Mr Darcy with him.

'It is a very fine day – why don't we all go out walking?' Mr Bingley suggested.

Mary was busy with her piano practice, but the others agreed at once. Bingley and Jane were soon dawdling behind arm in arm, talking happily together of their wedding and their future home,

leaving Elizabeth and Kitty to try and entertain Mr Darcy. None of them had very much to say to each other and, not enjoying the walk much, Kitty said she was going to call in at the Lucases' to see Maria.

As she hurried off down the lane to Lucas Lodge, Elizabeth was left alone with Mr Darcy – and made up her mind to take this opportunity to say what had been on her mind ever since she had received Mrs Gardiner's letter.

'Mr Darcy, I must thank you for your kindness to my sister Lydia,' she began awkwardly. 'Ever since I have known of it, I have been anxious to tell you how grateful I am.'

Mr Darcy frowned at once, and Elizabeth added hurriedly, 'You mustn't blame my aunt for telling me. Lydia gave it away, and then I couldn't rest until I knew exactly what had happened. Please, let me thank you on behalf of all my family, since they do not know what we owe you.'

'If you will thank me, let it be for yourself alone,' said Mr Darcy simply. 'Your family owes me nothing. Much as I respect them, I believe I thought only of you.'

Elizabeth was too flustered by this to say any more, and for a long moment, they walked side by side in silence. Then Mr Darcy said, 'If your feelings are still as they were in April, tell me so at once. My affection for you – and my wishes – are unchanged.'

Elizabeth barely knew how to reply. 'My feelings . . . they are so different,' she managed to say – and Mr Darcy gazed at her, his usually haughty expression completely transformed by an astonished and delighted smile.

There was so much to think and feel and say that Elizabeth barely noticed where they were going. For once she didn't pay any attention to the countryside around them as they walked, for she could only think of Mr Darcy. They talked and talked over everything that had happened, and she soon learned that she had Lady Catherine to thank for Mr Darcy's decision to propose to her again.

'When I heard about her visit, I began to feel hopeful,' admitted Mr Darcy. 'I know you well enough to be sure that if you had been absolutely decided against me, you would have had no problem in saying so to Lady Catherine.'

Elizabeth laughed as she replied. 'Yes, you know enough of my frankness to believe me capable of that! After speaking so rudely about you to your face, I could have no scruples about being rude about you to your relations.'

'But I deserved everything you said about me,' said Mr Darcy, shaking his head. 'I can hardly think of the way I acted without feeling ashamed. I remember how you told me that I should have behaved in a *more gentleman-like manner* ... you have no idea how those words have tortured me.'

'I had no idea that they would ever be felt in such a way,' said Elizabeth.

'You said that I could not have proposed to you in any possible way that would have made you willing to accept me,' remembered Mr Darcy.

'Oh! Do not repeat what I said then!'

'I have been a selfish being all my life,' said Mr Darcy seriously. 'As a child I was taught what was right, but not to control my temper. I was spoilt by my parents, who, although good people themselves, taught me to be selfish and proud and overbearing – to care for no one but my own family, and to think badly of the rest of the world. And so I might still have been but for you – dearest and loveliest Elizabeth.'

Talking in this way, they walked on and on, going for several miles. Mr Bingley and Jane were quite forgotten about, and when at last they returned to the house, Jane's eyes were wide. 'Where *can* you have been all this time?' she asked in surprise.

'Oh, we were just wandering about,' said Elizabeth hurriedly.

But when she and Jane were at last alone together in Jane's bedroom later that night, she told her the truth.

'You are joking, Lizzy! *Engaged* – to Mr Darcy? No, you are teasing me! I know it must be impossible.'

'Oh dear,' Elizabeth laughed. 'If you don't believe me, Jane, I am quite sure that no one else will! I'm telling the truth – Mr Darcy still loves me, and we are engaged.'

Jane's face was doubtful. 'But Lizzy, it cannot be – I know how much you dislike him.'

Elizabeth shook her head. 'That is all forgotten now.'

'Can it really be so? My dear Lizzy, I congratulate you. But are you really certain you can be happy with Mr Darcy?'

Elizabeth saw that Jane was concerned, and tried to explain how she felt. 'There can be no doubt about it. It is all settled between us that we are to be the happiest couple in the world. I am afraid you will be angry with me but I must admit,

I like him even better than Mr Bingley!'

But Jane just shook her head. 'Lizzy, be serious. How long have you loved Mr Darcy?'

'It has been coming on so gradually that I hardly know,' Elizabeth admitted honestly. Then she gave a mischievous grin. 'But perhaps . . . I believe I can date it from first seeing the beautiful grounds at Pemberley!'

The next day, Mr Darcy came with Mr Bingley to see them once again, and this time when Mr Bennet withdrew to his library, Mr Darcy followed him there. Elizabeth knew he was going to talk to her father about their engagement, and felt rather agitated, unable to imagine how Mr Bennet would respond to the news.

A little later, she found him alone, pacing up and down in his library. 'Lizzy!' he exclaimed on seeing her. 'What are you doing? Are you out of your senses? Have you not always hated Mr Darcy?' He shook his head in astonishment. 'He's rich to be sure, and you will have more fine clothes and carriages even than Jane. But will he make you happy?'

'Have you any other objections – other than your belief of my indifference to him?' asked Elizabeth.

'None at all,' said Mr Bennet. 'We know he is a proud, unpleasant sort of man. But that wouldn't matter if you really liked him. I have given him my consent. He is the kind of man to whom I should never dare to refuse anything. But let me advise you to think better of it, Lizzy. Let me not have the pain of seeing you unable to respect your partner in life.'

For once, Elizabeth was solemn in her reply. 'But I do respect him,' she said honestly. 'And I do like him. I love him.' She went on to explain how much her opinion of him had changed, talking of his kindness, and his generosity, and explaining what he had done for Lydia.

Mr Bennet listened in amazement. 'This is an evening of wonders! So Darcy was the one who found them, gave Wickham the money and arranged for his new position? I should never have dreamed of such a thing, If all this is true then, well, he deserves you. I could not have parted with you to anyone less worthy, Lizzy,' he said. Then he grinned at her. 'Now, if any young men should come for Mary and Kitty, send them in – I am quite ready for them!'

As for Mrs Bennet, she was so astounded by the news of Elizabeth's engagement that she sat quite still, unable to say a word for several minutes, which was certainly an extraordinary occurrence.

'Good gracious,' she said at last after some time

had passed. 'Mr Darcy! Who would have thought it? Oh, Lizzy – how rich you will be. You will have a house in town, and everything that is charming. Jane's is nothing to it, nothing at all!' All at once her  opinion of Mr Darcy had changed completely. 'Such a charming man – so handsome – and so tall. *Ten thousand a year!* Oh my dearest love, tell me what dish Mr Darcy is most fond of, and I will make sure we have it tomorrow!'

Elizabeth feared it would all be rather embarrassing, but when Mr Darcy and Mr Bingley came to see them again the next day, Mrs Bennet was so awed and excited by her new son-in-law that she could barely say two words. As for Mr Bennet, Elizabeth was pleased to see that for once he stayed out of his library, instead making great efforts to get to know Mr Darcy better. That evening, after Darcy and Bingley had gone, he came and sat beside Elizabeth.

'Do you know, I believe I am going to like your husband just as much as Jane's,' he said seriously. 'Although of course,' he couldn't resist adding with a wicked grin, 'my favourite son-in-law will always be Mr Wickham.'

# CHAPTER TWENTY-FOUR

Mrs Bennet could not have been happier on the day that Jane and Elizabeth were married. Their husbands were everything that she had ever imagined in her wildest dreams.

But although he liked both Mr Bingley and Mr Darcy, Mr Bennet could not feel quite so cheerful. While it was true that Jane would not be very far away at Netherfield, he knew that he would miss Elizabeth very much indeed – though he was already looking forward to visiting her in her new home at Pemberley.

In fact, Jane and Mr Bingley only stayed at Netherfield for one more year. After a little while, being so close to Mrs Bennet became trying even for Jane's good nature, and they decided to move to a new home not far from Pemberley, which meant that Jane and Elizabeth could see each other often. Elizabeth could not have wished for anything better than to have her sister close by.

Meanwhile, while Mary was happily left at Longbourn with her books, her piano and the opportunity to say exactly what she liked without any interruption from her sisters, Kitty paid lots of long visits to both Jane and Elizabeth. But though she was often invited to visit Lydia, who wrote to her promising balls, parties and the chance to meet lots of young men, her father would never give her permission to go.

As for Wickham and Lydia themselves, they did not bother to attend the wedding. But Elizabeth did receive a short note of congratulation from Lydia, which also mentioned that she and Wickham did not have quite as much money as they would like, and could Elizabeth and Mr Darcy possibly arrange to send them another three or four hundred pounds a year?

Lady Catherine did not attend the wedding either. She was so outraged when she heard the news that Mr Darcy and Elizabeth were to be married that she wrote her nephew a furious letter, and for some time refused to have anything to do with him.

On the other hand, Miss Bingley *did* attend the wedding – though Elizabeth's sharp eyes did not miss the fact that she looked very sour indeed throughout that happy day. But she was so fond of visiting Pemberley that she was forced to be polite to Elizabeth, and to congratulate her on her marriage, even if it was through gritted teeth.

Mr Darcy's sister, Georgiana, could not have been more pleased to have Elizabeth as her sister-in-law, and they soon became the very best of friends. Mr and Mrs Gardiner came to see them all very often at Pemberley, and prided themselves on the part they had played in bringing Elizabeth and her husband together. For as Elizabeth had written to Mrs Gardiner soon after she and Mr Darcy had become engaged:

*I thank you again and again. For if you had never taken me to Derbyshire, who knows what would have happened?*

*I am the happiest creature in the world – happier even than Jane. She only smiles, I laugh!*

But even though Elizabeth was very happy indeed, perhaps the happiest of all was Mrs Bennet.

'Three daughters married!' she said with a satisfied sigh. 'Oh, Mr Bennet, I don't believe my poor nerves shall ever trouble me again!'

# A NOTE FROM KATHERINE

I was twelve when I discovered Jane Austen for the first time. That year my best Christmas presents were a hardback copy of *Pride and Prejudice* and a video cassette of the BBC TV adaptation, starring Jennifer Ehle and Colin Firth as Elizabeth and Darcy. I watched it so many times I could recite it by heart – and to this day I still think it's the very best screen adaptation of the book.

# ✳ JANE AUSTEN ✳

My friend Felicity and I both fell head over heels in love with the story of the Bennet sisters. We adored Austen's colourful characters (dastardly Wickham, awful Mr Collins and haughty Lady Catherine de Bourgh), the glorious Regency world of balls and country houses, and especially the romance between Elizabeth and Darcy. We were forever quoting our favourite lines to each other: 'Are the shades of Pemberley to be thus polluted?'; 'Go to Brighton? I wouldn't trust you as near it as Eastbourne!'. We even used to write each other long letters in the characters of Elizabeth and Jane.

I went on to read all of Jane Austen's books, but *Pride and Prejudice* was always particularly special to me, and it's a book I revisit often. Retelling this much-loved story was a daunting challenge, but also enormous fun. It's no surprise to me that it has inspired lots of other retellings – from modern interpretations (*Bridget Jones's Diary* by Helen Fielding), to retellings told from the point of view of different characters like the Bennet family's servants (*Longbourn* by Jo Baker) or youngest sister Lydia (*Lydia* by Natasha Farrant) and even a horror version (*Pride and Prejudice and Zombies* by Seth Grahame-Smith).

This version of the story has been created specifically with younger readers in mind. If you've enjoyed it, I hope you'll one day go on to read the original novel, so you can fall in love with the delicious wit and cleverness of Jane Austen's writing for yourself.

# A NOTE FROM ÉGLANTINE

My name is Églantine Ceulemans, and as you might have noticed thanks to my first name . . . I am French!

In France, we tend to associate Britain with wonderful English gardens, a unique sense of humour, William Shakespeare and, last but not least, Jane Austen!

It was such an honour to have the opportunity

to illustrate Jane Austen's stories. I have always enjoyed reading books that are filled with love, laughter and happy endings, and Austen writes all of those things brilliantly. And who wouldn't love to illustrate gorgeous dresses, stunning mansions and passionate young women standing up for their deep convictions? I also tried to do justice to Austen's humour and light-heartedness by drawing characterful people and adding in friendly pets (sometimes well-hidden and always witnessing intense but mostly funny situations!).

I discovered Jane Austen's work with *Pride and Prejudice* one sun-filled summer, and I have such good memories of sitting reading it in the garden beneath my grandmother's weeping willow. This setting definitely helped me to fall in love with the book, but it would be a lie to say that I wasn't moved by Elizabeth and Mr Darcy's love story and that I didn't laugh when her mother tried (with no shame at all) to marry her daughters to all the best catches in the town! I imagined all those characters in my head so vividly, and it was a real pleasure to finally illustrate them, alongside all Austen's other amazing characters.

Jane Austen is an author who managed to depict nineteenth-century England with surprising modernity. She questioned the morality of so-called well-to-do people and she managed to write smartly, sharply and independently, at time where women were considered to be nothing if not married to a man. I hope that these illustrated versions of her books will help you to question the past and the present, without ever forgetting to laugh … and to dream!

# SO, WHO WAS JANE AUSTEN?

Jane Austen was born in 1775 and had seven siblings. Her parents were well-respected in their local community, and her father was the clergyman for a nearby parish. She spent much of her life helping to run the family home, whilst reading and writing in her spare time.

# ✳ JANE AUSTEN ✳

Jane began to anonymously publish her work in her thirties and four of her novels were released during her lifetime: *Sense and Sensibility*, *Pride and Prejudice*, *Mansfield Park* and *Emma*. However, at the age of forty-one she became ill, eventually dying in 1817. Her two remaining novels, *Northanger Abbey* and *Persuasion*, were published after her death.

Austen's books are well-known for their comedy, wit and irony. Her observations about wealthy society, and especially the role women played in it, were unlike anything that had been published before. Her novels were not widely read or praised until years later, but they have gone on to leave a mark on the world for ever, inspiring countless poems, books, plays and films.

# AND WHAT WAS IT LIKE IN 1813?

## WHERE DID PEOPLE LIVE?

The well-off lived in townhouses or grand country manors but those in less fortunate financial positions lived in small, overcrowded houses where whole families would often squeeze into one or two rooms. The really poor or orphaned might live in a workhouse. You could tell a lot about a person's family from how large their home was, and how much land they owned. Mr Darcy's house and grounds show just how well-off his family was.

At this time, property was always passed down through male heirs – so daughters could risk losing their home if their father died before they were married. This helps to explain why Mrs Bennet was so eager for her daughters to marry rich men – she would have been very worried about the possibility of their family home passing into the hands of Mr Collins, who was the closest male heir, before the Bennet sisters had comfortable homes of their own.

## WHAT CLOTHES DID WOMEN WEAR?

Women wore lightweight dresses with scooped necklines, over the top of several layers of undergarments. These dresses were usually white or pale in colour. Wealthy women wore more colourful dresses, often adorned with ribbons and embroidery. Hats were a must when outside, and women would personalise their bonnets to their own individual style – you might remember that right at the start of *Pride and Prejudice*, Elizabeth is trimming a new hat, and that later Lydia talks about how she has bought an ugly bonnet with plans to make it prettier herself.

## WHAT CLOTHES DID MEN WEAR?

Men usually wore white shirts and full-length

trousers, tucked into knee-length boots or leather shoes. Those with money or higher social status wore waistcoats and long tailcoats over the top of their shirts. They also wore hats; top hats were the most common style for wealthy men.

## HOW DID PEOPLE TRAVEL?

Walking was the most common form of travel, but for longer distances riding on horseback or using horse-drawn coaches was common. However, this came at a price that many could not afford. Just like cars, there were cheaper and more expensive coaches – Lady Catherine's barouche would have cost a lot of money.

# COLLECT THEM ALL!

### Jane Austen's EMMA
WITTY WORDS BY KATY BIRCHALL
DELIGHTFUL DOODLES BY ÉGLANTINE CEULEMANS

### Jane Austen's PERSUASION
WITTY WORDS BY NARINDER DHAMI
DELIGHTFUL DOODLES BY ÉGLANTINE CEULEMANS

### Jane Austen's SENSE AND SENSIBILITY
WITTY WORDS BY JOANNA NADIN
DELIGHTFUL DOODLES BY ÉGLANTINE CEULEMANS

### Jane Austen's MANSFIELD PARK
WITTY WORDS BY AISHA BUSHBY
DELIGHTFUL DOODLES BY ÉGLANTINE CEULEMANS

### Jane Austen's NORTHANGER ABBEY
WITTY WORDS BY STEVEN BUTLER
DELIGHTFUL DOODLES BY ÉGLANTINE CEULEMANS